THE ARRAN

A VEGAS BILLIONAIRE ROMANCE
CHARLOTTE BYRD

BYRD BOOKS

Copyright © 2016 by Charlotte Byrd

This book is a work of fiction. The names, characters, places and incidents are products of the writer's imagination or have been used fictitiously and are not to be construed as real. Any resemblance to persons, living or dead, actual events, locales or organizations is entirely coincidental.

All rights reserved.

No part of this book may be reproduced in any form or by any electronic or mechanical means, including information storage and retrieval systems, without written permission from the author, except for the use of brief quotations in a book review.

CONTENTS

Acknowledgments

About The Arrangement (Book One)

PART 1

1 Grant

2 Grant

3 April

4 April

5 April

6 April

7 APRIL

8 Grant

PART 2

9 Grant

10 April

11 Grant

12 April

13 April

14 Grant

PART 3

15 April

16 Grant

17 April

18 Grant

19 April

PART 4

20 Grant

21 April

22 Grant

23 April

24 Grant

25 April

26 Grant

29 April

FREE EXCERPT: The Debt

Chapter 1

Chapter 2

Chapter 3

Chapter 4

Chapter 5

Chapter 6

Chapter 7

Chapter 8

Chapter 9

Chapter 10

Chapter 11

Chapter 12

Advanced Reader Team

Books by Charlotte Byrd

ACKNOWLEDGMENTS

Dear Reader,

Thank you so much for taking the time to read this book. Without you, I would not be able to do what I love. Your support and generosity means the world to me.

I'm particularly grateful to my devoted and dedicated Advanced Reader Team and all of you who have read and reviewed the book prior to its official release. In particular, I'd like to thank Mary Wolney and Lindsey Leblanc who have gone above and beyond their duties as Advanced Readers. I love you!

If you would like join my Advanced Reader Team and get FREE copies of my books in return for honest reviews, please email me.

If you just want to let me know what you think about my book, please don't hesitate to write me. I love to hear from my readers!!

Love,
Charlotte

Dear Reader,

Each month I will be gifting 1 lucky reader a **$US 25 Gift Card (Amazon, Apple, Kobo, Barnes & Noble, etc - winner's choice)**.

Simply **leave a review** for this 'The Arrangement: Book One' on the retailer where it was downloaded and then email a screen shot of the review to contact@charlotte-byrd.com

The $US 25 voucher will be paid to the winner that will be randomly chosen, on or before **30th of each calendar month.**

Good luck!

xxoo

Charlotte Byrd

ABOUT THE ARRANGEMENT (BOOK ONE)

When April needs a date to her ex-fiance's engagement party, her friend sets her up with an escort. No sex. No strings attached. Just a hot guy who is paid to adore her for a weekend. What could go wrong?

Grant is a multi-millionaire and an escort. He doesn't do this for money. He can get any woman he wants, but he likes a challenge. You wouldn't think it, but women who pay for sex are so much more of a challenge. They aren't paying just for sex, they're paying for an experience. They want to be wowed and adored and pleased. And Grant specializes in all that.

At first, Grant thinks that April is just like the rest of his clients: curvy girl on the wrong side of 20 in desperate need of a mouth-watering date. But April doesn't want sex and she doesn't seem to want him at all. And Grant finds himself falling for someone for the first time ever…

PART 1

1

GRANT

Rebecca always strutted after our little visits, walking like a proud cat sashaying and swaying.

Pushing her hair behind her ear, I gave one last kiss good bye. It smelled just like the lilac in her bed sheets and coconut. Her skin was warm from the sun and made the whites of her eyes pop. She was incredible for her age.

"That tan is doing wonders for you." I told her, unlocking my Porsche as we stepped out of the French doors and down the slate stairs to the driveway.

"Let's hope that it takes more years off than it puts on later," she joked, showing her barely visible crow's feet as she smiled. "I can't turn 29 for a 15th year in a row." Rebecca combed the other side of her thick black hair behind her ears. She led me down the steps by her elbow and then slapped me playfully on the butt as I left, almost as if to say "good game". Her spirit was so young and playful, it made me sad that she was only a client sometimes. Then I would remember how insane she went during her divorce. It's better this way.

"Looks like you'll have to be 30 then. Lots of gorgeous women hit their stride in their thirties." I slid into the front seat of my car and began driving over the long stretch of driveway that separated her mansion from the road. I made a mental note to pick up a few flowers for her birthday next time I saw her. I'm sure that I would either make it to the guest list for her party or I would be the after party she had planned for herself.

My phone dinged that it received the funds from Rebecca, my favorite client. Her husband didn't know the great thing that he gave up. She was always a little more fun in bed than the others and she was more than willing to give me high praise. If I had a dollar for every time she told me I was better in bed than her ex I could probably buy a second car, maybe even buy a vacation home in the Virgin Islands.

The 30-minute drive from her house in Henderson to mine in Vegas was nice for reflecting. The sun setting in the sky didn't compare to the one that we saw over the weekend. I would have to travel back again.

I often think about how I'll avoid my parent's watchful eye, thinking up excuses for missing calls or texts. I always had to play just out of reach while still talking to them every so often. It's not that I don't like them, I just don't care for the way they yak in my ear, always nagging about me changing the way I work, having to listen to the "why can't you be more like your brothers" and other blah blah blahs. They cry that I should become a day trader again and put my degree to use, but I have enough experience in that to make money off the other day traders in my hedge fund. I always tell them that they shouldn't have raised me in Vegas if they wanted a respectable son. They don't think it's funny, and maybe it isn't meant to be. Maybe they should just appreciate the irony. They saw more problems with my life than there was. I was just happy to be happy.

Unluckily for me, they got three other sons that can put me to shame. I am always being measured up to them, and if I have to hear one more time about their accomplishments I will flip my lid. You think that they would have given up nagging me after high school, and then after that wasn't good enough maybe after college. I considered going to grad school to see if that was the finish line of the complaints. Finally I have decided that parents never stop parenting and they will always be somewhat disappointed in who I am, or rather who I am not: a business tycoon.

I don't do what I do for money, anyway. I do it for me. I was never really one to stick with interests in high school and college. I dabbled in almost everything and made a lot of friends on the way in each club, but I never really got hooked on anything in particular. You do things, practice, get good at them, and then what? Nothing. Well, there is one thing that it is nice to be good at. That's why I like being an escort. Each woman is different. Some like it rougher, and then there are some that need to be treated like tissue paper. Each client is different and I am very proud with how successful I am.

I can see my tan in the mirror from our getaway weekend to Mexico. Spending two days there put 20 grand in my bank account. Not half bad if you ask me. I keep my prices high to sort the pearls from the clams in this business. If I charged anything less than what I currently charge I could get mange or Black Death or cooties or something. It costs a pretty penny to be with me for a very good reason. It assured both skill and quality to my clients and reassured me that I was getting the very same back.

Pulling past the gate, I know there is only 5 minutes until I am officially home. They put so many speed bumps in a gated community to discourage people from driving around. It works pretty well, most of my neighbors have switched to bikes so their cars don't have to learn Braille in order to commute to work. There are certain things that you have to deal with when living in a ritzy part of the town of sin.

Really the longest part of getting home is the ride in the elevator up to my room. The penthouse is a billion floors up and there are several stops on the way between floors. People always forget this part in the movies, the downside with the glam. I have met a few clients in the past by hanging around the casino in the bottom. Since it's my dad's, all I have to do is get them a couple drinks on the house, slide my card over, and saying my line: "Your first win was getting this card, the next will be in that casino, and your third will be using my card with your new funds." It's cheesy and dumb, but that's Vegas. This is the light and the life that people come for.

Most of the people that work in this building feel one of two ways about me, they hate me or they love me. Some of that comes with me being the boss of them, the other part of their feelings has to do with me being the boss of me. No one likes playing by the rules, not even me. Fortunately for me, I'm not the one that has to worry about a pay check here.

The life of the bachelor was very different from what TV shows had made me believe. The day time can be fun, especially with my job, but the nights were very lonely. I could come home with women from bars, but I hadn't had a meaningful female companion in a long long time. Even just a friend would be nice, but I was surrounded by males. I think that since girls see that I'm sort of a smooth talker they think they can't trust me. They see this pretty boy exterior, but I really have more going on than just looks. I want to know someone. I want to feel like a kid again. Being an adult could be very boring. I'll save up all my escort money for a time machine.

2

GRANT

Here is where I decompress. After all the stressors of the world and people, I can come here and be sure that all things are the same, that I am safe from my parents, and that I can listen to my music as loud as I want, which is exactly what I did.

I flip on the stereo system as I walk in and grab a water bottle. This is part of the routine. In order to keep this body in shape staying hydrated is a must. You lose a lot of body fluids in the escort business, and that is the most vital part of being a human.

So checking my email regularly is a must in this business of service. "It's a business doing pleasure" is my motto. I take this as seriously as a doctor takes heart or brain surgery. I have to be thorough and efficient in order to keep my "I'm doing this for me" mindset. That's what my ego rides on, which is dumb and vain but sometimes it pays to be vain.

My first email is from my friend Alex and it's marked urgent, which sends up two red flags. The first one is "Why is my gay friend using my escort email to contact me?" and "Why is it urgent?" I have a very open mind set, but not enough to let my good buddy pay for a night with me.

G*RANT*,
You've gotta help me. I've got a lonely girl who needs you as an accessory to her at her ex-fiance's engagement party. It's Travis' roommate, and it would be doing me a solid.
Alex

I*T WAS SENT* one minute ago, so I decided to text him back that I would take the deal, I just needed to know how long I would be needed for. I met Alex in a very similar way to this. It isn't uncommon for young women to need a man to be a date for them. A large price to pay to rub it in the face of an ex, I guess. Alex was best friends with a girl who needed a date to a charity dinner, and we sat at a table together. There were many things he and I agreed on, and from there it has blossomed into a close and trusting relationship. He goes to the gym just as much as me and is around woman the same amount of time. If I were gay, maybe he would be the perfect guy for me, but for now Travis is filling those shoes.

Travis is also very cool. He is similar to both me and Alex, so I give him my approval. I haven't met him many times, since him and Alex aren't technically dating, they are just seeing each other with plenty of sex peppered in between interactions. I imagine they have a similar sex life to me, just with a lot less contract signing and credit cards scanning.

"A few days, not sure exactly how many. And her family will be there too."

"That all sounds fine."

"The only thing is, she is going through sort of a tough time, some kind of accident or something, I'm not sure what, I can get more details from Travis. He says that she won't be able to pay your usual rates."

I sighed and paused. I would do anything for a friend, especially one as good as Alex. The money isn't the priority for this job, but it's what keeps my standards high and makes sure that my clients have the same standards. "How cheap are we talking?"

"Her name is April. She thinks it costs $200 per night."

"Is she renting an escort or a birthday party clown?" For $200 dollars you could get a lot of things, a quality companion was not one of those things but many sexual diseases might be.

"I know, I know. I'll owe you big time. I wouldn't ask if this didn't sound like such a desperate situation."

"Okay, yeah, you owe me one. And this one can be free. $200 a night doesn't even cover my utilities here."

"She won't do it if she isn't paying. You could be homeless for all she knows. If she has to pay she thinks you're a decent guy." This was starting to shake up my night quite a bit. Maybe I could put this charity work on my profile.

"Could I talk to Travis about this?" Alex forwarded his number to me and I called.

"Hello?"

"So what kind of girl are we talking about? Is she 60 and riddled with herpes?" Travis snorted after I said this and excused himself.

"Sorry, I have to leave this room really quick. She was right next to me." Travis sounded a lot like Alex did but with a deeper voice and a lot less inflection. "April is a nice person. She's been in some trouble recently."

"It sounds pretty bad."

"You have no idea. Emotionally, physically, spiritually she is hardly the same girl I knew before the accident."

"What accident?"

"Minor car accident." He coughed out quickly. "Don't worry about that, we can get to that later. Point is, I'm the one paying rent most months, it's that kind of bad. She really is a great girl, but she just can't show up to her ex-fiancés' new fiancées' dinner alone and bent out of shape."

I sighed and nodded. "Yeah, I understand that." I'm no stranger to marriages. After all, this is Vegas. Marriages and remarriages happen all the time. I once had a client who had 5 different husbands below her belt. This kind of stuff isn't new to me. My parents even were both remarried, and happily so. I'm happy for them. I'm just still getting used to a new set of parents to nag at me.

"You can keep her money to cover her rent, think of it as charity or a gift from me on Alex. $200 really isn't enough to care about."

"Yeah, I know. I don't think she knows too much about the whole escort system." He snorted. "You guys can carve out more of the details later, I have to get back in there and lend a shoulder for crying."

"Alright, let me know if I can help in anyway."

"Thanks, Grant. I owe you one."

I clicked end and went back to staring idly out my window. The lights below flickered and blinked. It could make a seizure prone person paralyzed for life. I love this grimy, beautiful city. New tourists and people every day, different sketchy activities happening every minute, and the fresh smell of sweaty old gamblers and cheap hooker perfume was enough to make me feel at home.

I was always up for new adventures and challenges. This event sounded like it was going to be a fairly mundane and tame way to experience a wedding that I have no bias for. Maybe it would be healthy to spend a lot of time with a woman who isn't over a relationship. I could see what it's like to be attached to someone. I've never experienced this personally, but it looks wonderful from the outside. Well, until you get to the bad parts.

I've never had a healthy long relationship, and I've never been around one either. My parents were married for a long time, but it definitely wasn't healthy. They were always fighting and had nothing in common. I often wonder what actually brought them together in the first place, and I'm sure they wondered that too.

My brothers and I were all not surprised by the divorce. Several times they had separated and gotten back together, but it was final about the 5th time. They would cheat on each other and go weeks without seeing the other one. And then my mom met Mike and my dad met Tammy, and the rest was history. Not always happy history.

Tammy is pretty young for my dad. She's 32 to be exact. Dad has a type, and it isn't one in his generation. And now they're expecting a kid. When my mom heard, she practically moved into her plastic surgeon's office. She started buying vats of anti-aging cream and filled up her Botox punch card. And the fact that Mike is more than twenty years older than Mom also doesn't help matters.

Despite appearances, my dad isn't ecstatic about the new baby either. He isn't exactly young. Tammy could very well be the result of his midlife crisis, but that has come with some collateral damage.

I don't mean to be bitter. I do love my family as individuals, but growing up in a house with all of them wasn't a party. And it wasn't exactly easy. People assume that wealthy people have the most luck and are always having a great time just because we have nice clothes, nice cars and nice houses. But we're people. And people have problems. Even rich people.

Maybe that's what appeals to me about older women. They are straight up with you. They have had enough of men fucking around on them, so they aren't about to let some young prick tell them what to do. Things are simple with them. They say and do what they mean. No games. No bullshit.

Normally when I get back I would watch TV and catch up on the news, but I'm back late enough that all I can do is work out, shower and go to bed. Another one of the requirements for charging such a high price is being able to back it up with quality goods. I was always a little athletic but I had to make a very complicated work out and eating regimen to get in top shape for this business. I always made fun of those people that would eat a leaf of lettuce and then run ten miles a day, but sadly I have become one of them. I could conquer the high school prom queen at a non-eating contest.

I don't condone eating disorders. I think that they are horrible on a body and are a cry for help from anyone, but being disciplined is something different. If I weren't sculpted I wouldn't get the revenue and amount of return clients that I do. I don't like this side of me, but it's a side I have had to be honest about. No one is perfect, even if they try very hard to look it.

3

APRIL

"Stupid beautiful Isabelle and her stupid long legs." My fat around my stomach was soft to pinch in my fingers. I could see the stretch marks around my sides starting to turn from pink to white. "And stupid Tom and his stupid beautiful fiancé and their stupid happy picture on my stupid Instagram feed."

Travis came back in the room after his phone call and sat on the edge of my bed.

"I have stretch marks now, Travis."

"You know, those are considered beautiful in some cultures."

"Not helping. They aren't beautiful in this culture."

"No, really." He started brushing my brown hair with his soft fingers. "People call them tiger stripes. It's something you earn."

"That's if you get pregnant." I groaned and showed him the picture. "Look at these two stupid happy people."

"She is hideous." He lied, smiling over at me. "Not nearly as pretty as you are."

"You mean not as pretty as I used to be."

"April, shut up." That's what gay best friends are for: living with and telling you to shut up. Travis has been the nicest through all of these changes recently. He was the first to offer to find a new place with me, the first to lend me a helping hand (with some money in palm) and the first to actually visit me in the hospital. "If you really feel that bad about a little weight go to the gym."

"I have been going to the gym."

"Well, go more then. And eat healthy."

I sighed again and rolled over. My laptop showed that I had a new email from Cosmo. I had been waiting by my laptop day and night waiting for a reply to my article I submitted.

"Cosmo wrote back."

"Oh! Good news?"

I opened the email. "Nope. They rejected it." Apparently "How to please your man in Bed" was an overused topic and it needed more zest in order to be published. I groaned again, as that seemed to be my communication method.

"I bet dumb Isabelle doesn't have a bad day at work."

"What does she do?"

"Dumb executive assistant for a dumb Universal Studios hot shot. Hopefully they have an affair and call off the wedding. And then dumb Tom can go to dumb Google and do whatever dumb thing he gets paid for and be unhappy at work."

"This dumb wedding." Travis jabbed at me. He left my room and let the door creak behind him.

"I bet she doesn't live in a dumb ugly apartment" I muttered under my breath. Normally I wasn't this ungrateful, I couldn't even afford this apartment with how freelancing had been going as of late. Pasadena isn't exactly cheap and the landlord won't take my fat as payment.

"Wait, where are you going? Can't you see I need you?"

"Sorry, doll. I have to go to this dumb audition to make dumb rent." Travis was an actor, and supposedly a good one at that. Maybe that could be my next career move. I can play everyone's fat best friend. "I'll come home right after. We can get dinner and I'll bring wine or something."

"Make it arsenic, or maybe just rat poison will do."

"Never lose that sense of humor, April."

And with that he was gone. I turned the TV on and tried to do some crunches while watching a reality show. Realities shows were great for making me feel better about having a personality and being a decent person while simultaneously making me feel horrible about my body. I often did a quick workout routine when watching TV since I wasn't up early enough to do those morning yoga shows.

After I was all crunched I flipped open my laptop and skimmed through all the freelance jobs available. I preferred article writing, pop culture and feeding into it really is my strong suit, but at this point I would take any job that is offered to me. I have written vacuum reviews, made lists until my brain has fallen out, and still I am too broke to pay for anything.

This apartment is nice enough to live in but not nice enough to stay. As soon as I get a regular paying job Travis and I are out of here and into somewhere where the water comes out of the faucets completely clear and the paint isn't chipping off of the ceiling. I will miss the inspiration that all the characters we live next to give me, but I won't miss their loud banging or arguments or the elephants that live upstairs.

I often think about moving away from the west coast, or at least just out of California. I don't think that will ever happen though. It was hard enough to leave Santa Barbara when I had to. I was born and raised there, as was dumb Tom. Why does my family have to be friends with his family? How do you friend break up with a whole group of people that have been there through diaper changes and growth spurts?

You don't. And you can't. The Middletons were closer family than some of my aunts and uncles. I should have known better than to have fallen in love with someone so close to everyone. They were there for the accident, but that caused the collateral damage of my un-engagement. Life has been more glamorous for me before than it is now. At least I worked off some of the extra weight.

I got in this car accident. I'm fine now, but I was bed ridden and put on heavy pain medication for a while. I gained 70 pounds, and I have lost 30 of them. I'm still 40 pounds heavier than I want to be, and I've been at a plateau for a while now.

I did another set of crunches in between applying for different article writing gigs. Hopefully some magazine would take as much pity on me as I have.

4

APRIL

Even when I'm not eating, sometimes my brain default thinks about food. It makes it incredibly hard to keep the weight off and even harder to not just give up all together. I didn't have much money, the accident put me out of work for a while, so I was struggling to get by to a point where food was scarce. I didn't have the stamina to get a part time job on the street but also had too much pride to ask my parents for help. It didn't take a therapist to recognize that I was a mess. This is the lowest point my life had had, and it was affecting every aspect of living.

After the accident I couldn't eat or sleep, and talking was even difficult. I had been driving home from a concert at night. It was a really really good day. I am thankful for that, that it was at least a great last day to have. While flipping through the stations on the radio a drunk driver coming from the opposite direction had gotten in the lane just enough to bump me. When I tried to turn the car, and keep some of it from bashing into the other drivers I over adjusted and turned it right into a tree. I was going 60 miles per hour, the other driver was going 80. He spun out and went down hard into a ditch. They tried to revive him for a few hours after, but eventually either he lost the will to live or his BAC got the better of his body.

Even though I was the victim of that accident I had a tremendous amount of guilt. I was upset the other man died. Even if he was being a jerk, I didn't want his family to have to deal with that loss. I was sure he was going through something bad if he had been driving after drinking. They said he was three times over the legal limit and almost bound to die anyway. When his parents visited me they told me about his life. He had found out that his wife had been cheating on him. He didn't want to tell anyone, he wanted to keep it from his kids so that they could work it out in private. She wouldn't admit to it and it drove him mad, making him unsure of what to do. That night they had a huge argument and he was going to finally decide to break it off. His mom was crying very very hard. She was upset that he made a dumb decision. She said he had talked about how depressed he was, and how he almost didn't have the will to go on. She had wished she had listened better and gotten him a therapist.

When I learned all of this instead of making me feel better it made me feel much worse. I thought of him a lot, especially after Tom called the wedding off. I should have seen it coming. He had never wanted to set a date. We had dated for six years before that, all through college and then after graduation. We were happy with each other, but when we lost the spark I knew that the engagement was a way of trying to fix a broken relationship. I swore we would both get over it, that all couples go through this kind of thing, and most do. And then it all changed with the accident. I saw him less and less. He talked stopped talking about our future, and stopped talking to me. When he broke it off I thought maybe he just needed some time away. Maybe my accident was causing us both to be depressed. It was depressing him, but he didn't want to fix things. Instead he started a dumb new relationship last June with lady long legs.

That's why the worst part about all of this was the collateral damage. I gained the 70 pounds because I was bedridden and almost addicted to painkillers. As I healed I was dealing more and more with problems in my personal life, and one thing that was always there for me no matter what was food.

When he left he never really left my life. My parents had known the Middletons before I had ever met Tom. When we started dating it just made them better friends. They all swore that it was destiny or part of some greater plan. I was foolish enough to believe it. We had a good time at the University of San Diego. I loved that he was different than me. I was incredibly expressive, I tried auditioning for plays and graduated with a major in English and Creative Writing. Tom was a Computer Scientist.

We were really exciting to each other. He kept me thinking critically and taught me a few new things about the computer. If I ever wanted new software or couldn't figure something out I had a professional on standby. When it came to computers I was about as useful as an 80-year-old Grandma that lived on a desert island. He liked that I was artistic and that I was a little bit insane. He told me all the time that I was the most exciting girl he had ever met.

The more we got to know each other the less we had in common. The less we had in common the harder we had to try to make it work. Six years was a really long time to be dragged along. You don't get dragged that long without severe carpet burns and an excellent sense of what the bottom looks like. He probably felt the same way. None of our friends liked each other. One of the few friends of mine left was Travis.

Travis came in the door, envelope in hand, waving it above his head. I quickly tried to make it look like I wasn't laying like a lump on the floor.

"What's in there?"

"My check from that commercial a month ago," he sang, skipping into the kitchen. Travis had worked with one of the local companies on making a commercial. He had to do really cheesy dialogue and it would air overnight, but it was still acting. He swayed back and forth, probably texting his boyfriend about the money.

"Congrats!" I was very happy for Travis. He was getting a lot of work and doing really well in his field. It made me feel pathetic when I saw his progress in an almost impossible job field and my lack of progress in the easiest field of work.

"So what are we eating tonight?"

"Air. I don't have money. I can look at your food, though. Sniff it a little maybe." I crawled back onto the couch and hid under the blanket. "This will be good for my diet. Being broke might be the best thing to happen to me."

"If you don't start cheering up I am going to force feed you cocaine." Travis shot me daggers from his eyes. He was very motivated, happy, and athletic – my exact opposite. Instead of it helping me live a healthy life style it made me more upset at myself. "I just got paid. Dinner is on me."

"You really don't have to do this, Travis. You've done too much for me."

Travis walked over to the TV and changed it to the Food Network. "Yum. Look at all that. Maybe we should have Chinese. Maybe Italian. Ooh, how about sushi?"

"Did you ever study methods of torture?" The food on the television looked divine. When your will power is low but your bank account is lower it is hard to pass up free food. "And let's get salad or something. I really don't need something heavy."

"You deserve good food. You already lost 30 pounds. That's amazing. You should be congratulated."

"I have had enough congratulations."

"Well, not from me." Travis sorted through our cabinets of take out menus.

"How does Italian sound?"

"It sounds like the most delicious thing ever."

"Great, it's settled."

"No, wait!" I thought about my diet. "Isn't that super heavy in carbs?"

"Okay, not Italian. How about Mexican?"

"Too greasy."

"What about Thai?"

"Aren't noodles heavy in carbs?"

"It's food, so yes. Do you want to eat paper?"

"I don't want to stay fat."

I was not having the best day, but I was trying to be more positive. It was hard with the wedding and debt.

"If you want I can help train you. We can get you back in shape. Then if freelancing doesn't work out, maybe you still have some acting skills that we can get you jobs with."

"Maybe."

"Let's start by walking to get Thai."

5

APRIL

"I'll just have the water, thanks." We sat at a table by the windows. It was a gorgeous night out. All the beautiful people were out walking, enjoying the sunshine and shopping. I envied them. One day I would have a life style that was hopefully close to theirs. I wanted to be able to write, for fun and for work. I wanted to have a nice condo or house. I wanted to have enough money to buy a meal.

"No, we will each have a glass of Moscato." Travis handed the menu back. This guaranteed that I was only going to have a salad. "Alex told me that this place has the best white wines."

"How is it going with Alex?"

"Best sex I have ever had." That was enough in Travis' book to be marriage material. He was practically a sex addict. He didn't let it take over his life, just drive the motivation for it. "How is your freelancing going?"

"Not great. I've been broke for God knows how long."

"Two months."

"Two months. I am thinking about giving it up and looking for other work."

"Ooh, like what? Stripping?"

"Not with this muffin top."

"Where are you going to work, then?"

I took a large drink of wine. It was almost like a juice. "I was thinking maybe doing something more mainstream. I sent my resume out to a few administrative assistant positions. I did some secretary work at USD so hopefully that is enough experience to get me into one of them."

"Have you heard back from any of them?"

The waitress brought our food out. "Not yet." My life was sadder on paper than it felt. I was sitting across from a great guy that maybe if he weren't gay, I would date him. Too bad for me, he already had a boy toy.

"Well, you have to keep at it. Persistence is key. I don't do acting full time. It hardly pays the bills."

"You'll make it soon. You're getting a ton of work."

"Yeah, it's going well right now, but it hasn't always been this way. That's why I still work as a hostess. Someday I won't have to show people their tables; I'll just be able to become characters."

"You'll make it soon."

"You just said that." We ate the dinner and I was stuffed afterwards. Travis insisted we get dessert, but I couldn't fit another bite in me. We went back out and walked around the plaza area.

"So how about this wedding thing?"

"And just when I got it off my mind."

"Sorry. I just don't want you to show up empty handed. You're walking now, that's the first step. We can get you hot before then. You can't show up empty handed."

"I know."

"You'll be a laughing stock."

"I know."

"You'll look pathetic."

"I know."

"They will all feel so bad for you."

"Hey, yeah. I get it."

"So how is the dating situation going to work?" Travis and I walked into one of the boutiques. He looked at all the shoes, showing me several pairs he thought would look great on me.

"Well, still single. My closest male friend is a gay guy that Tom would know I'm not dating."

I tried on a few of the heels. I was happy that they didn't break under my weight.

"We can't all have ourselves so figured out. And it's not like I have many lady friends to choose from either. Maybe I should just fake sick and stay home."

"They will feel even worse for you."

"It's better than facing them."

"That's too bad." Travis' hand breezed over some fabric. "Just when I had an idea."

"Oh?" I was beginning to get excited. I could see some of these dresses being perfect for the wedding, the empire waist slimming down my stomach and pumping up my boobs.

"And don't get mad about this."

"Uh-oh."

"So Alex has this friend."

"Okay."

"And I think he could be a great solution."

"Get to the point. Who is he?"

"Have you ever heard of an escort?"

"Oh my god."

"Hear me out."

"No."

"He is really hunky."

"No."

"And he could probably get you a discount."

"Oh my god no." Is this what I had become? Unable to get a date for myself and having to pay for a man to spend a weekend with me? Curling up into my bed forever had never been more appealing, not even when I was bed ridden. "I would rather die."

"Don't be so dramatic."

"What if they knew him?"

"Then you would know that they pay for sex and you would have a leg up on them." Travis handed me a few dresses. I wanted to throw them all at him. I wanted to hide in the racks like I was a kid again. When was my life going to stop going down hill?

Maybe a therapist could help me with all of these things. Travis was great to talk to. He always comforted me and told me the truth. He wouldn't sugar coat things, he knew that that was what I needed to hear. I had enough time being coddled by my friends in the hospital. He was the one that kept me realistic and reminded me that things would get better, even if they kept getting worse. That didn't mean I didn't hate him when he was telling me the truth.

"That would make me want to die. I want to die. Kill me."

"Shut up, April. Try this on. It's your color."

It was my color. It made me look slim. Maybe if I kept my hair down and contoured a lot I could look like I used to.

"Is he hot?"

"He gets paid to have sex. I would hope so."

"I would too."

"Do I hear you considering this idea?" Travis sang from outside the dressing room.

"Definitely not." He tossed a few more dresses over, I could already rule out a few of them. "These are all too low cut."

"Show off your new boobs."

"That's a bit trashy."

"No it isn't. But it will make him upset he didn't stick around for them." He slid some shoes under the door. "We have to get you a makeover. You'll need a push-up bra or two."

We walked back home, twenty minutes there. We passed several beautiful people and too many of them were couples, holding hands. For too long I believed in true love. I wanted to play red rover and run through their locked fingers. I was already old and cynical but only twenty-seven. I was going to age fast and become a very bitter lonely old lady. I wish I liked cats. Then I would have something to love. Now I was just a failure of a freelancer and even bigger failure of a writer. My professors all said I had promise, but I didn't see any of that.

When Travis and I got back we popped in a movie. I couldn't pay attention to it, too much was going through my mind. It was getting harder and harder to find joy in simple daily things. I couldn't even watch a movie without it reminding me of all the stresses in my life. Travis kept drinking wine and steadily became very tipsy. Eventually he passed out on the couch. I wish I had a bottle of wine. I wish I could fall asleep like a rock.

I checked my email again. No new messages. I looked online for job postings. Maybe I could just work at McDonalds to pay the bills. Once I made actual money I could get a liposuction or maybe buy diet pills that actually worked.

6

APRIL

My room was really warm and I curled up in my bed. This was the safest place on earth for me. I could hide here forever and be okay. My phone vibrated in my pajama pocket. It was my mom, the last person I wanted to talk to. I answered it anyway.

"April, dear, you look awful."

"Thanks mom."

"Sorry. Are you sick?"

"No. I'm just not wearing makeup."

"Oh... Well..."

"It's nighttime, mom."

"Doesn't mean you should stop trying. I wanted to see how you are."

"Not just make me feel awful?"

"Of course not. You know I care. I was there the whole time you were broken by that awful drunk driver."

"I know, mom."

"Which was over a year ago. It's never too late to get back in shape, honey."

"I already feel shitty enough, mom."

"Sorry, sorry." She fell silent for a moment and straightened her dress. "I'll change the subject. I will be going to a garden and tea party tomorrow. Guess who will be there."

"Who?"

"Mrs. Middleton. That woman took my month to do it. She knew it was my turn to host, and yet here she is. As if the wedding wasn't party enough for her." My mom and Tom's mom were the kind of friends that hated each other. I heard enough of it when I was together with Tom, hearing it when I was lonely was much worse. It served as a reminder of my past.

"I don't even think I can go to that wedding, Mom."

"What!?" My mom began messing with her hair frantically. "You must. There is no way you aren't going to this party. They stuck with you when you were in the hospital, it's the least you could do."

"I feel bad enough for not going, you don't have rub it in my face too."

"You're going. If you don't go they will know you are still upset, and then they will blame me, and it will be an absolute mess."

"I really don't want to go a fat, lonely slob."

"The Middletons are our oldest friends. You aren't going to ruin our friendship with them."

"You and dad don't even like them anymore. You were just bitching about her."

"Watch your language."

"Sorry."

"And your father still likes Roger."

"No he doesn't. They argue all the time."

"It's like politics, dear. They are having lively discussions."

"No, they argue about dumb things like who knows more about what and what is the classiest this and that."

"That's politics."

"I don't think a friendship would be ruined if I couldn't make it to a wedding party."

"Clearly you don't know the Middletons anymore."

I sighed. I really didn't know them anymore, but I had known their family well enough when I was on my way to be part of it. There was no arguing with my mom, she always had to be right, another thing that her and Denise had in common. They should be best friends. I quickly tried to change the subject. I didn't want every time I talked to my mom to be having to hear her complain and nag. She was only like this because I wasn't at home for her to keep a close eye on. I never really got to see her, and I saw my dad even less. "I miss dad."

"He misses you too, honey. Want to talk to him?"

"If he is around."

My dad popped out from around the phone corner. "Hi, honey!" I was a little embarrassed that he had heard all of that.

"Hi, dad."

"How is life?"

"Okay."

"Just okay?"

"Yeah, I'm kind of broke. And I haven't been getting any work freelancing."

"Oh, that's too bad, sweetie. You can always follow in your mom's footsteps."

"What's that?"

"Sit around and use my money. Join the family business." I laughed and my mom smacked him away.

"Shut it, Roger. Tell your daughter she has to go to the wedding."

"You have to go, April."

"But why?"

"Because they are our friends and they are nice people. I know it is hard to see Tom, especially after everything. Doesn't it make you happy enough to know that he is happy?"

"No. It makes me miserable."

"Aw." Both my parents sighed. My dad left the frame and left my mom to help, which wasn't any help at all.

"Wouldn't we all be happier if we just stopped being friends with that family all together?"

"Probably."

"Great! Then that's the plan." My mom shook her head and sighed.

"No way. We share the same social group. I know that Denise would use her little blabber mouth to spread rumors about what I have said about them."

"Then maybe you shouldn't complain about them to her."

"Well, it's too late for that. And these are my friends too. She can't just steal them like she stole my spot for the garden party."

"I don't even have a date."

"You don't need a date, you have your dad and I."

"I can't show up to my ex-fiancés wedding alone."

"Sure you can."

"Would you?" She got silent again and then left the room, going into her reading room.

"No, I probably wouldn't."

"Then why should I?"

"Because I'm your mother and I said so."

"I'm twenty-seven."

"And you're going. And that's that."

"Your logic is unparalleled, mom."

I missed my mom, as much as she helped me feel bad about myself. We had a lot in common. She had also been left by someone. He was the man just before my father. She claimed she didn't love him, that he didn't really mean that much to her. It was someone that she had known since childhood. Their parents had paired them together. Supposedly they were inseparable as kids. My grandma said that they grew more and more distant the older they became. After the engagement he decided that he wanted to follow his dream of moving to Europe. My mom was against this idea but was willing to travel if it meant following him. Then he decided he wanted to go to Africa, and when my mom kept offering to follow him he decided to tell her that they were through and that he had met someone else. My mom hates talking about it. My grandma said she was sick for months after it, unable to eat or sleep. I knew just what she had been going through.

"If you don't go we will be very disappointed." I assumed my mom might have had some sympathy on me, since she had been through the same thing.

"Fine, I'll see what I can do."

"Thank you, sweetie. We can send you some money to help you through this month. I'll see if I can help find you a job."

"Thanks, mom. But I'm not happy about this."

"You'll forgive me."

"I guess."

"We will have a good time."

"I doubt it."

"Well, I'm going to get going before you can change your mind. I'll talk to you again soon."

"Bye mom."

"Bye, sweetie." My phone clicked off and I stared at my wall for a while. I didn't want to move. I didn't want to go to the wedding. The less I did the slower time moved. It seemed I had run out of options. I was either going to have to find a magic lamp to rub in the next few days or I was going to have to talk Travis' hooker.

I can't believe I was stooping this low. I feel so pathetic. This is nowhere near where I thought I was going to be at this time in my life. I could tell my parents were disappointed too. If any of my professors had found out, they would probably be nice but also doubtful of a future for me. I didn't have any connections to work off of. I didn't have as much as I did when I was in school. I was fat, single, and broke, the three least desirable traits a person can have.

I never thought in my life I would come in contact with a sex worker, let alone hire one. Meditating on this for a while I knew I had no other options. Maybe I could Facebook an old boyfriend from high school, or maybe I could fake my own death and run away to another state, or maybe another planet. I could become a hermit and demand squatters rights and panhandle for trade.

My phone felt hot in my hands. I typed out the message. "If I have to go to this wedding, I'm not going to go alone." I sorted through my dresses in my closet. Hopefully my parents would send me enough money that I could buy a new one. My fat clothes didn't fit me as well, and my skinny clothes would probably never fit me again. Even my shoes felt weird on my feet. I was another person trying to squeeze into the shell of someone else, the past me, a much smaller and happier person.

7

APRIL

Why do I have a body to take care of? I can't afford the food it needs to survive or the gym equipment it takes to make it look decent. Lucky for me, Travis has one of those deluxe gym packages, which means he gets to bring one friend with him. Normally he just texts me pictures of all the hotties working out here, but now I was going to be able to feast my eyes while fasting my body.

I wasn't very excited about being so lonely I had to hire a prostitute as a date. I couldn't help the present circumstances, and I didn't want to be cut off from my family. At least I could feel better about my body if I was the one that was shaping it. Travis showed me his routine, which was something impossible for my body to endure. Instead he wrote down a light workout for me, since this was my first time.

"So this is what I have to do this week?" The paper was front and back, and there were some terms on here that I didn't understand. I would need to get drawings too. Maybe a diagram.

"That's for today."

"Are you trying to kill me so you can use my room as a closet?"

"You know how I feel about closets. If I liked them, I wouldn't have come out of the one I was in." I was unable to laugh looking at this impossible list of deeds. I wouldn't have been this worried if he had handed me a ransom note and my mom's pinky toe.

"So how much of this is English?"

"Oh! Hold that thought. I just saw a hunk walk into the sauna." Travis left me. I figured I might as well start with what I knew. I hopped on the elliptical and searched my phone for games to use. Maybe this would be a good time to get acquainted with my most expensive date.

Hi. Is this Grant? I texted.

I started kicking forward. For whatever reason I felt more awkward now talking to him than I had ever felt talking to a crush or boyfriend. Maybe it was because we were strangers or maybe it was my brain screaming at me for dating a hooker. In high school I was voted most likely to succeed, and if I told this story at my next reunion I doubted I would live it down.

Yep. Who is this? He wrote back almost immediately.

April. Travis gave me your number. I'm the girl looking for a wedding.

Ah, yes. Hello, April. Tell me about yourself. He wrote.

I huffed as I ran. My eye stayed glued to my phone screen. I didn't want any of these people to look at me. What they saw was a fat girl trying to get into shape but what was really happening was a broke fat girl trying to get hot for a fiancé who had dumped her and hiring an escort to make him jealous. As if I couldn't go any lower in the public's eyes.

Can we can do that when we meet in person?

Of course.

Where do sex workers do business? A coffee shop like normal people? Maybe a bar? I should probably just treat this like a date. Our first date of few to follow.

Where do you live? He texted.

I finished a mile. Only a billion more to go. The calorie burning count wasn't nearly as high as I felt it should be. This was going to be a lot more work than I intended.

Pasadena, I texted.

I'm from Vegas. The city of sin.

Go figure, I thought.

That's a little far away, I wrote.

But I'm in Santa Monica right now for a few days. On business.

My heart started to thump and all the blood drained from my face. Oh my God. This is actually becoming real. And then suddenly, something occurred to me. What if I had to pay for his travel expenses. Shit.

I can't really afford to pay you anything beyond the date, I texted.

No worries. Just meet me in Santa Monica and don't worry about any billing.

I kept running and had a new found motivation. I wanted to be at a point in my life where I didn't have to hire someone to hang out with me. I wanted to be able to sit at a restaurant with a man that wasn't gay who genuinely found me attractive and funny. Maybe I would have to give it up and become homosexual myself, but until we got to that bridge my biggest hope was to date excellence and shove it in Tom's face. My phone vibrated again.

How about surfing? He texted.

It's okay, I guess, I wrote. I didn't really have any opinions about it one way or another.

No, I mean, do you want to go surfing?

My heart skipped a beat. Of course I didn't want to go surfing. Not with this body. Everyone would think I was a beached whale and try to roll me back in the ocean. Maybe I would actually prefer that. I really didn't want to go out though. I only had bikinis from the thinner days.

I don't think that's the best idea, I wrote desperately trying to come up with a plausible explanation as to why not that was not the truth.

I have an allergic reaction to salt water, I finally texted. Is salt water allergy even a real thing?

Oh, I'm sorry to hear that.

Yeah, it makes me all red and puffy, I added.

Great. Now I looked like a big nerd too. There should be an app that texts for you or at least prevents you from being incredibly awkward and off putting.

It's a skin condition, I explained further even though any explanation would've been enough.

How long had it been since I had a first date? I couldn't remember the last time I was single and in the dating pool. I was so young; it was just before college. I wasted all my years with Tom, and so now I have no experience. How do you flirt? Does he pay if he is my hooker? Do they have discount cards? I was already going to have to pay 200 dollars a night for a few days.

This wedding was the lowest I would be. I should just call my mom and ask her if she would rather me come to the wedding with a hooker as my date or if she would rather me not go at all. Which would really be more embarrassing for her?

I entertained the idea of calling it all off again. I couldn't stand the idea of everyone seeing me flounder. I didn't want college to be when I piqued. I didn't want to pique. I wanted to have a successful job, or just a job in general. I wanted to be able to walk into that reception and show everyone that I kept the boobs and butt but slimmed down my stomach. I wanted to wear a dress that gave Tom a boner and made him wonder why he ever dumped me. Who dumps a car crash victim? Losers who lose great girlfriends.

I felt sort of bad for hating Tom's new fiancée. She might have been nice and maybe she didn't mean to murder my heart. Maybe she didn't know she was a home-wrecker until they were into each other. The thought made me sad. What didn't I have that she had? Other than a job and a body. I had more time with him than her. That should have been enough to secure our relationship for life. I stopped feeling bad for her. She was the reason I was single. She was the reason I had to hire someone to go to her dumb wedding. I would be nice to her, but I would not like her. My mom couldn't even make me do that.

Thinking about all this pushed me faster and farther on the elliptical. I was running at a very fast pace and my heart rate monitor was skyrocketing. Maybe I could do this every day. I did the math in my head. If I ran 5 miles every day I would lose about a pound each week. There wasn't enough time to get me back to my start body, but it wasn't too late to give some effort. I would have to eat healthy and go on a huge diet. This was going to be the turning point. No more feeling sorry for myself. No more asking for pity. I would go out there, find a job, a boyfriend, and I would get hot. This would be a new and improved April. Positive thoughts only.

So, how about lunch at one? Grant texted.

I waited and thought out my text before I replied to him. I switched to a weight machine and worked my abs. How many crunches would it take to get me a hot body by the time I have to go on this date?

It was currently 10 AM. I had enough time to finish this work out, spruce up, and get over to Santa Monica in time for a lunch date. I was glad I still had enough make up. I would have to contour the shit out of my face before I saw this man. I'm sure he already thought I was probably hideous. What 27-year-old needs to hire someone as a date? This 27-year-old. I flipped through a Cosmo as I waited for Travis to be done. I needed flirting and dating tips to really rub it in Tom's face. He would fall for the facade of my new glamorous life. If I tried hard enough maybe I would too.

Sounds good, I finally texted back.

8

GRANT

There is nothing I would like to do more than jump into that crystal blue water. It was calling my name. I missed this when I was away in Vegas. I wish I had more clients in California just for this sunshine and beach. I could happily be homeless living here.

I have to admit I was disappointed that April didn't want to surf. I loved to surf, and it would be my favorite hobby if I could regularly do it. I had enough time here that I could get some surfing in, but not as much as I liked. It's never enough for me. When I was at USC I would spend all of my free time on the waves. There was a simple pleasure about feeling the wake on your board. The smell of the water was divine. Riding a wave would take me out of my element. It almost didn't matter if I stayed on the board or not, to be tossed in was still just as fun. It was a marvel to see the inside of a wave breaking. It sent a rush through me like no other.

It was hard to experience adrenaline like that now. When I was out working I was always feeling a little guilty towards my parents, thinking they wasted their money on a failure as a kid. When I was away from work I was actually a little lonely. Hobbies like surfing would keep that off my mind. I would cure it if I could, but very few respectable women want to be serious with someone who is an escort full time. I tried not to think about it. I had plenty of company from both clients and friends. Sometimes people just yearn for a little more than that. I've been feeling that yearning a lot recently.

I pushed it out of my head. It was no use thinking about. April wasn't very familiar with coffee shops in the area, so I chose one that I knew catered to my diet. I had to eat light today since I was taking someone to an awards show tonight. I'm not disclosed to say who, but she recently got out of a relationship.

She wasn't ready to start dating again, even though she is attractive and friendly and could have had anyone. I was glad she chose to do business with me. It isn't a totally radical idea for someone wanting to use my services just for dating. Odds were, though, that it ended with something a little more than just a kiss goodbye. Having known this client for enough time before, I would say that my chances of getting lucky tonight were high. If I were in Vegas I would raise the bet. Luckily for me there is no opponents, only a dealer. Either way I was leaving with a heavier pocket.

When April walked in I was a little surprised. She had told me that she would be wearing a black maxi dress, one of the most popular items on the beach today, but I knew this was her. She had a sun hat and sunglasses that she took off when she stepped in. Something told me about the way she carried herself she wasn't very confident. I had no idea why. A curvy girl like that could get tail around her any night. I would even sleep with her for free. I pretty much was. I waved to her and she came and sat across from me. She took very elegant strides when she walked. Travis had told me her family was stuck up, I was only hoping that she wasn't. With the way she walked with a classy step, something told me she might be.

"Hi." Maybe I was wrong, though.

"Let me get your chair for you." I stood up and pulled out the seat. I was in the business of wooing women, but something about this girl was wooing me. I almost wished we had said dinner instead of lunch.

Even just drinks would have been better. Her pearly whites beamed. I'm sure the allure of being around someone my own age was all that this attraction was, but it was real. My primal instincts were yelling, telling me that her eggs were still fertile. My silly balls and their desire to have a baby against my will.

"Thank you." She sipped her water and refused to make eye contact. I could understand that. Meeting a date for a first time was hard enough. I had grown too used to this business, and I could tell I was probably going to do most of the talking. Surfing was still on my mind.

"It's too bad we couldn't enjoy the ocean. You should really get a medicine or something. Today's weather would have been perfect." She coughed while swallowing her water. Did I say something wrong?

"Yeah, sorry about that. We can sit outside if you want."

"No, we can just walk later. Maybe grab a drink." The waitress brought our coffees and I was eating my words.

"Okay. So should we talk terms?" She pulled out a notebook and wrote "Wedding Business" at the top of the page. She made a list called "Expenses" and wrote my name down.

"It will be $200 a night. Sex will be extra." She wrote that down and kept her eyes on the page.

"That won't be a problem." She wrote down another checklist for a dress and shoes.

"We will just see about that." I said that, mostly joking. But who was to stop me from coming on to her. If I had to act the part, I could do a very convincing job. It might even help convince her family. She stopped writing and put her pen on the table.

"No we won't. There will be no sex. There will be no extra charges."

"Okay." This was starting to be one of my less comfortable meetings. I felt a bit flustered in her presence. I wasn't sure why. Her self conscious manner was rubbing off on me. "Should we order?"

"Sure. I'll have a chicken Caesar salad. Ranch dressing."

"I'll have the same, hold the dressing." I took a drink of my water and waited for my coffee to cool. She picked her pen back up and started writing her lists again.

"I've never met a straight man who eats salad."

"I have to go to an awards show tonight. I can't really afford to eat anything else. I am on a very strict diet for these kinds of things."

"That sounds really glamorous." There was an element of surprise in her voice.

"Yeah, I'm going with an actress. You aren't the first person to hire me as a date. It's actually not that uncommon, so you shouldn't feel too bad."

"What makes you think I feel bad?" This girl was very on edge.

"Sorry, I didn't mean to assume anything. Travis just told me that times were tough recently." Her face went from harsh to soft and she finally met eyes with me. Her irises were gorgeous. There were small spirals of several different colors. They were green with a ring of bright brown that was almost orange. I had to catch my breath. If it weren't for her sour attitude, I might have complimented them.

"No, you're right. I'm sorry." She started drinking her coffee. "This is just really nerve wrecking and not how I wanted to go back to see... My friend."

"I understand." We sat for a while, not saying much. There was a bit of a wait since we arrived at the prime lunch time. "So what do you do in your free time? What should I know about you? How can I be a realistic date?"

"Oh, yes, good idea." She ripped a page out of her notebook and handed it to me. This girl was very type

A personality. "You need to read this. It has a low down on what you should know about me. My family doesn't know that you're a hooker –"

"Escort."

"Escort, sorry. They are already ashamed of me as it is. No offense. I don't think them knowing would help any."

"Don't worry about that. I know all about disappointing your parents."

"Then we already have a lot in common." This woman was funny, without always meaning to be. I wanted to see her again. It was probably just my hormones going crazy along with my desire to surf. I had a lot of nostalgia for the beach, and it could make these things complicated and awkward if I did too much associating. I just had to remind myself that it was just business and that at least I wouldn't leave empty handed.

The waitress brought our salads out and I read over the list. "So where are we going?"

"I wrote that stuff on the back. I will pick you up at the airport in Santa Barbra around one on Friday. The engagement party is on Saturday. There is a list of the types of clothes you should bring."

I laughed and she looked surprised. "Sorry, I just figured you would assume I know what to wear to a wedding." She smiled back and started picking at her salad.

"Sorry. I'm just a bit obsessive. I have some nervous tendencies. I don't want a single thing to go wrong this weekend. I hardly want to be there at all."

"That's an expensive date just to keep up with appearances."

"I'm doing it mostly for my mother, and believe me, I know." She ate more of her salad before continuing. "So do you do checks or just cash?"

"I actually have an app for all this. It's pretty simple. I also have a contract I need you to sign." She seemed relieved that there were official papers. She struck me as rather odd and very nervous. I could tell that she wasn't used to meeting strangers. "Whose wedding is this?"

"My ex-fiancé's."

"Ouch."

"Yeah." She stopped eating her food after that and stuck with the coffee and the water.

"Don't worry. We will stick it in his face." I was trying to comfort her. I wasn't that good at emotionally comforting women. I mostly just did the physical stuff.

"Once he sees that you have a hot boyfriend he will regret giving you up."

"Fake boyfriend."

"Right."

"But we have to make it look real."

"I understand."

"If they know that I hired you..." She started repeating herself. "Then I will be dead to the world."

"We wouldn't want that."

She went back to eating and I ate my salad too. I could see her frequently check around the restaurant to make sure that she didn't know anyone there. The only way to get figured out that you are with an escort is to act like you don't want to be seen with one.

"What else should I know? You don't have your job on this list."

"That is an excellent question." She ordered a glass of wine. I ordered one for myself as well. "I don't have a job." She started laughing at herself. She was a little crazy, but I like that about her. Quirks could be good. It would take a lot of the attention away from me this weekend.

"So your parents don't know they are paying for me? That's a little naughty."

She laughed again and almost swallowed all her wine. "They shouldn't have forced me to go to the wedding if they didn't want their girl to turn to the streets. It's their own fault."

I decided to pay our bill. It was obvious she already had enough on her plate, and maybe it would make up for me offending her earlier. She left and I was able to ride some waves. I liked the way my hair felt after the salt water soaked it. While I was surfing I couldn't keep my mind off of her and her peculiar habits. It was obvious she was suffering from some body hate. Maybe a little get away with an experienced man like me was all she needed.

PART 2

9

GRANT

I wasn't expecting a limo or anything to pick me up, but I found it comical to see April pull around in an old Dodge Neon. It was black and the perfect car for someone like her. You could tell she adored that thing by the way it had seat covers and a steering wheel cover too. She fidgeted a lot, fixing her make up in the mirror. She scraped the smudged parts away, the ones that were too microscopic for my eyes. I could see heavy bags under her eyes. It was clear to me she didn't get much sleep the night before. April was probably worried the whole time. This would either be a great weekend for both of us or it would be a horrible one.

I feel like the polar opposite of this girl. While I am organized and well groomed, she cares a lot more about her parents' approval than I ever pretended to.

With the way she picked at her nails I could tell she was anxious to see them. Or maybe she was anxious to see Tom. I bet this whole weekend was going to make her go from crazy to a basket case. She hummed along with the radio and told me to put my luggage in the back with hers. All her suitcases were miss matched, and each seemed to be from a different era. I wasn't sure how long we were staying there, but with the amount she had packed it looked like an eternity. This wasn't uncommon for women. This really wasn't uncommon for women who were trying to say "fuck you" to someone.

"So are we moving to Santa Barbra after the wedding?" I joked.

She looked confused, gazing back and forth between me and her luggage.

"What do you mean?" She asked, cautiously.

"You just have a lot packed."

"Oh. Yeah, I know. Sorry. I never know what to wear to weddings." Maybe that is why she assumed I didn't know what to bring. I snickered to myself and she seemed a bit uncomfortable.

"You're fine. I've had clients who have brought more for less."

"This is a weird request. Could you stop bringing up your old clients as of now? It makes me feel weird."

"Yeah, sorry. I wasn't going to do it in front of your family or anything."

"No, it's for me too. I don't want to be part of the type that is referred to as a client."

"Suit yourself." She pulled out onto the highway and we were off. The car was a stick shift, and as I saw her changing gears I noticed that she was wearing a t-shirt and sweatpants. She really didn't know what to wear to these events, but I never thought she was the laid back type.

"You're dressed pretty casually." I said. She took note of my suit and remarked back. She was one of the few women I knew that still wore make up when wearing sweat pants and a t-shirt. I wasn't complaining. She looked comfortable, and I was a little envious. I was also too professional to wear those clothes to attend to a client. Everything I wore was business professional. I took myself very seriously, even if my parents didn't. It was about pride more than about image. I needed people to know that I did this job as a way to make myself happy, not as a way to make money. This woman had me feeling a little funny, though. Not that I didn't enjoy it, it just made me feel strange and nervous like most clients don't. I guess that probably was an age thing, as well. I didn't have much experience with serious dating, and having to act like I did this weekend was going to be a bit of a difference for me. Shouldn't be too hard to handle, though.

"And you seem a bit over dressed."

"I always dress to impress. If you don't want to be seen with me, I have to make it so there is nothing to complain about." That wasn't true. I normally dressed nice for clients, but I wasn't going to say that again. When I said that I could tell she was more embarrassed than annoyed. I felt bad. Normally people took my snide remarks as jokes. I saw she was internalizing it. "I'm sorry, that was uncalled for. I've just had a rough day."

"Yeah. Airports will do that to you." At least she was understanding. "So what is our story? What should we tell my parents? Last I spoke with my mom, I kind of told her how I was pretty single, so we should come up with a good excuse."

"How about you just didn't think I was ready to meet the family yet. After all, it is awkward to bring a new boyfriend around your ex-fiancé's wedding."

"That's a good point. Okay, so we aren't that official yet. We have been dating for six months."

"Make it two. Six months is verging into serious territory."

She nodded in agreement. "Okay yes. We have been dating for two months." As we drove, I couldn't help but stare out the window on her side. She noticed and looked back at me. "What? Why are you staring?"

"Just looking at the ocean." I wasn't. I was admiring the warm afternoon sun on her face. I saw how it reflected and danced on her eyes.

"Yeah, it's lovely out today. I can't wait to swim."

"I thought you couldn't touch salt water?"

"I can't. I meant at the pool." She flipped the station to the CD and started singing along with one of the songs. "So how did we meet?"

"I saw you at the bar. I thought you were the most beautiful person to walk into the room. I ordered you a glass of wine, and you sat with me. We talked until the bar closed and they had to kick us out. Apparently you knew my friend Alex who was dating your roommate Travis."

"Dating is a big word. They are more friends with benefits territory."

"Okay, where did you go to school?"

"I attended USC. Valedictorian."

"Excellent, my mom will love that."

"And where did you go to school?"

"University of San Diego."

"That's a good school." She struck me as bright. "And your major there was?"

"English, and I'm a failure at it. I haven't gotten a single job."

"In time you'll find something."

"Let's hope. And it better not come with an apron or spatula." I laughed at her joke. She was taken back. I was really surprised she didn't know how funny she was. She smiled over at me, warming up I hoped. "So when they ask what your career is, what do you say?"

"I will tell them that I flip burgers with you."

She laughed and then told me no a thousand times. "Okay, what will you actually say?"

"I will say I'm in finance."

"Ooh, that's good. Then they will think you have money. That could be my motivating factor for dating you."

I knew that it was just internal dialogue, that she was trying to make our story, but this still was able to sting a little.

"Maybe they will stop harassing me about getting a job and will just keep sending me cash so they don't think I'm using you. Maybe I can tell them that too.

That we had a fight because you thought I was taking advantage of you. Yes, okay good." She was mostly babbling to herself now and I was still looking back between her and the ocean. "Okay, what kind of finance do you do?"

"I run a small hedge fund."

"Eh, that's good, but it isn't super believable."

"It's what I actually do." I fished in my wallet for a business card and handed it over to her.

"What?" She looked between the road and my card. We pulled into the hotel and was thrown back. "Really?"

"Yes. I didn't have those made just for this weekend."

"Wait, I can't tell if you are serious or not."

"Call the number if you don't believe me." I got out and started to unload both of our things. Travis told me that Tom was really nice, but he didn't seem like the best guy if he broke up with a girlfriend of six years after a car accident. It also seemed so recent to April that I didn't really understand why Tom would already be engaged. Maybe April really was crazy. I'm sure this weekend would give me a better feel for her personality, whether I wanted it or not.

I almost had that list she gave me memorized. I knew what to do and what not to do. I could tell that she was the type to be easily agitated, but I have worked with this type before. It seemed so strange coming from someone so young who supposedly had their life in shambles.

I had actually been to this hotel before on business. It was very nice, and I could tell that not only did she come from money but she was expected to marry into money. The poor woman's life must have been very foreign and scary for her. I could understand that, even if I never experienced it. I gave her the benefit of the doubt because I thought she was adorable. She was a little curvy and spoke her mind without thinking twice of stepping on someone's toes. I made a mental list of her quirks. So far I had nail biting and picking at it as well as excessive list making. And inability to dress for an occasion would have to be added also.

April was an enigma. A lovely type A-anal enigma.

I'm sure I could win her over. She won me over without trying.

10

APRIL

I could feel adrenaline pumping through me as we pulled in. I wasn't used to lying to my parents, especially not about something this big. I knew they would expect more details. I wished we had had more time in the car to go over things. Grant was being fairly nice, but I wasn't ready to spend time with him just yet.

I put the business card he gave me in my wallet. Maybe later I would check it out, see if it went to his voice message, but for now I had other things to worry about. I worried about my parents. I worried about the hotel. I worried about money. I worried about carrying my luggage up. Before I knew it Grant had tipped the valet and took our suitcases out.

That was baffling. He had given the boy a seemingly large tip and I wasn't expecting to see him spend a cent. I guess that is part of the money I gave him. It might as well be going to something good. Grant pushed our luggage inside. I felt like this was over kill but I didn't mind. If I was going to pay that much for him I was going to make him work for it.

I could tell he was a little on edge too. I'm sure that even though he posed as a boyfriend for several people, he probably never had to go to a wedding. I don't think that that was part of his values. Actually, I'm sure that is the exact opposite of his moral values. He didn't strike me as a hooker at all. That's probably why he used the word escort. I'm sure it wasn't all fun, after all he was already hot but still had to order only a salad. He didn't even get a dressing. I was having a hard enough time and it had only been a few days. I didn't want to live life in his shoes.

He opened the door for me as I walked in. I couldn't tell if he was just a gentleman or if he was laying it on too thick. I decided not to mind it too much. If Tom saw this he would know that this is how I should have been treated. I should have been shown nice things and I should have had chivalry thrown at me like a fish at a farmer's market.

This hotel was ritzy and gorgeous, just like I would have expected my wedding's hotel to be. I could tell now why Grant was dressed nice. I was embarrassed again but tried not to let it eat at me like it used to. I had already noticed a few people looking at me funny and decided that sunglasses were a good idea.

"Room for April Somerset." I said. As the front desk person turned around, they greeted Grant with a firm handshake, ignoring me.

"So nice to have you with us again, Mr. Taylor!"

"How many times do I have to tell you to call me Grant?" Grant's smile could light up the whole room. He was incredibly charming, and was apparently nice to all workers, not just people in charge of handling a car.

"Let us take your luggage up to your room."

"That won't be necessary." They handed Grant the cards and told him to give the manager of the bar a certain card for free drinks. Grant leaned over and asked me if there was an open bar at the ceremony.

"I'm not sure."

"We might need this after all, then." He tucked it in his shirt pocket. I felt like a fool in my clothes, but at least I was seen with a high roller. As long as they associated me with him and didn't compare us, I felt like I would be doing fine.

"Make sure no one finds out about your little job."

"Everyone knows I run a hedge fund." Grant eyed me as if to keep me from screwing myself over. Maybe he had more experience doing this than I gave him credit for. I was starting to get excited, apart from seeing Tom and his walking stick fiancée. If I could pull this off I could have a nice dirty little secret to take with me home as a souvenir. I had a whole new level of secrecy to swear people to.

He seemed much smarter than I gave him credit for, and he was incredibly friendly. I was trying to pick at him and find some flaws. It was getting harder and harder. I kept noticing my gaze focusing on his shirt, trying to find the outline of his abs. I can't get carried away. I can't sleep with him. This is just business. It isn't worth the extra cash or the complication. I straightened my shirt out as we rode up the elevator, all our bags in a cart.

We got to our room on the 8th floor. I was a bit upset as we stepped inside. I forgot to call ahead and ask for a double. There was only one bed in this room, and I didn't feel comfortable enough to share. I didn't think that over. That must have been the one detail I over looked. I hoped it was the one detail I overlooked. What else could I be missing? I sat at the edge of the bed and picked at my finger nails.

"So I made a mistake."

"What's that?"

"This room."

Grant looked around the room and tried to understand what was wrong. "What's missing from this room?"

"A second bed. I forgot to call ahead. I'm sorry. We can get a second room. I'm sure I could find a way to charge it to my parents or something."

"I don't think that works with our story. Not unless you have stingy parents."

"Oh."

"So do you have stingy parents?"

"No, not really."

"So don't worry about it."

He wheeled our clothes in and put my suitcases on the floor. His followed and he began unpacking. I decided that as long as I'm here, I'm going to try to enjoy it. At least this room has a balcony. I could get some peace and quiet there. If things got bad enough, I could even jump. Was eight stories enough to kill a person?

"Aren't you going to unpack?"

"What?" I turned back from the balcony to see all his clothes moving from his suitcase on the bed to the top drawer of the dresser. "Oh, no. I don't unpack at hotels."

"Why not?"

"It just means more packing up. It's not like I wear everything I pack."

He looked at my three suitcases and nodded. "Yeah, I guess that makes sense to me." He was chuckling as he finished unpacking. I don't know why it was so strange to this man. I'm sure he frequently stayed at hotel rooms with women where no clothes were touched other than the ones that they threw off onto the floor. I didn't understand him. He didn't seem like he was judging me, or at least it felt like he didn't have the grounds to. I hadn't done any wrong to him. Well, except for lie about a skin condition, but that was it. I turned back to look at the ocean. It did look inviting. Maybe I would come clean, just so I could take a dip in it. It had felt good to be bad, though. I liked the thought of having a naughty weekend. I liked thinking that I was doing something that my parents hated without them knowing. I liked not having the consequences of an escort with all the advantage of a boyfriend. I was going to make this weekend my turning point. This is where I would start living life for me and by my own rules. I would please my parent this last time, and then after this I would give up caring what they thought. I was going to be the April of my internal desires and fantasies who didn't take no for an answer and stopped letting people walk all over her.

"So what's on the agenda? Just stay snug in this hotel room?"

"No, there will be an informal cocktail tonight. It will be on the terrace, so it should be a great view of the ocean. It's for all the guests who are flying in tonight."

"You mean your parents are purposefully putting you through another day of misery than they need to?"

"No one ever accused them of being nice."

"Yeah, that's unfortunate." He changed ties and looked back at me, eyeing my outfit.

"What are you going to be wearing tonight?"

"Oh shit. I'm not sure."

"Well, we have to match a little. I have some other ties if this one doesn't match. What dresses do you have?"

All of them. Travis and I had gone shopping yesterday. I hadn't lost much weight, but I was starting to get a tighter waist. To celebrate he took me on a bit of a spree, and we bought everything except for the store they were in. I could feel myself beginning to panic. I went back to gnawing on my finger nails. "I don't know. I don't know. What colors do you have? What do I wear?"

"Calm down." He walk towards me and put his hands on my shoulders. I hate to admit it, but it did help me feel better. "How about you just show me what you've brought. That way we can decide together. Maybe it will help your confidence."

"Okay, yeah. Maybe you're right."

"You don't have a rash or anything do you?"

What a weird question. I was going to rebut but then I remembered the supposed skin condition of mine. "No. I don't have a rash."

"Okay, good. So there shouldn't be a problem with what you wear."

We were able to take out a lot of the dresses and limit it to three. One of them was a nude and black striped dress that had an empire waist and mock neck. It was floor length and probably the one I felt the most comfortable in. Dresses this size were like portable blankets.

"That's good, but what else do you have?"

The next one was a knee length dress that made me feel regal. It was burnt orange and had a boat neckline. It was fairly plain other than the tuxedo paneling on the sides.

"Okay, what else do we have?"

This last one was the one I was the most terrified to try on. It was one of those classic "little black dress" dresses. It was slinky and fit me tight without being too snug. The neck was a deep plunge and showed off my newly pushed-up boobs. It was backless and required I wear either lace or nothing as far as underwear went.

"Gorgeous. This is the dress. I'll wear this silk tie."

"I don't think I can actually wear this out."

Grant stopped sorting through his bag and went to sit next to me. "Why, what's wrong with it?"

"It shows off too much."

"Are you kidding? This shows off the perfect amount. This dress is sexy while still being classy. This dress is bold. It hugs your curves, and it will drive him crazy. He will stay awake at night wondering why he ever left you. This is the dress that make men fantasize and women jealous."

He was right. I should probably wear this dress if I wanted to make him jealous. It looked good on me, like really good. It looked like I hadn't gained any weight in the first place. If I was going to be the new April, this would be the dress to wear tonight.

"Are you sure that striped one isn't better?"

"That one is gorgeous, but this one is drop-dead gorgeous. Trust me, I've seen some beautiful women and this puts them to shame." I couldn't tell if he was being nice or genuine. I felt like he was hitting on me. I tried to keep myself from falling for him. It's hard when someone is cute, nice, handsome, and supposedly very wealthy.

"Okay. Wear that tie. I'm going to do my hair and makeup." I put on a smoky eye and curled my hair back. This was the most I could do without needing a crew to help. I stepped back out of the bathroom, make up done, hair done, and dress on. I saw his eyes. His draw literally dropped. He was being so sweet. He did one of those slow spreading smiles and I could feel my confidence slowly growing back.

"They say you aren't supposed to wear white to a wedding, but they never warned me about black."

"I can't speak right now, you're so gorgeous. How did I get this lucky? How did you need a date?" He did a cheesy wolf whistle and made me laugh. I was blushing a lot. I could just say it was my makeup. The little nagging voice in my head reminded me it wasn't real, no matter how good it felt. I wanted it to be. I want to feel this good forever.

11

GRANT

Of all the people in the world to need my service, she was without a doubt the most room stopping. I couldn't take my eyes off of her. It was going to be impossible to come up with an excuse for staring at her this time. Her soft brown hair was swept neatly to the side and curled, and her eyes could melt even the coldest mountain. I could feel myself swooning a bit. I had to stop.

She loved the attention. I saw her blush and become happy. I didn't know how a woman this gorgeous got to be so self conscious. If she weren't a client I would kiss her right now and try to keep her from leaving the room the whole night. If she was a car, I was a deer standing in the headlights.

"Close your mouth, you're leaking drool." She giggled. I loved her giggle. She had a soft sweet laugh. I was becoming more and more excited to spend this weekend with her.

"You look ravishing. You look enchanting." I remembered why we were here. "You're going to knock him off of his feet." I tightened my tie and offered her my arm. "Shall we go down?"

"We shall." She took my elbow.

As I walked her to the elevator I could feel my body telling me that this woman was different from the rest. It wasn't just age difference anymore, and it wasn't the fact that she was adorable. There was something about the way she was peculiar that I loved. Maybe she would continue to see me after this weekend. I'm sure I could put her dead-beat ex to shame. He was going to rue the day he split up with her. This whole wedding was going to be asking "what happened between you and April" to him. He would have nothing to say other than "I've made a huge mistake."

I could tell she felt good. At first she was hiding when she put this one, but once she got into her high heels and make up, she was beginning to see what I saw.

"So I'm going to meet your mother and father tonight?"

"Yes. Hopefully you won't have to do too much talking. They have a lot of nagging at me to do anyway."

"Right. Okay. So we met at a bar and you were wearing this dress."

"We didn't agree to that."

"Let me fantasize." I felt like I was making her uncomfortable with my bluntness. I wanted her to feel beautiful, but I didn't want to be off putting.

"Save it for when there are people around."

"You're a person too, April." Maybe I should have waited to shmooze. I didn't want to come off as a horny escort, even if that is what I was. I just wanted to make sure my client had a good time, and if we had a little more fun than the contract required then it was all for the better. The elevator opened and we went into the terrace.

"Okay, here we go." She said, squeezing the handle tight. We entered the room, and just as I thought it would happen, everyone was stunned. It could have been shock about seeing the ex-fiancee, but I knew better. It was seeing someone like this in person. It was intoxicating. "Oh no, here comes my mom."

Just then a pompous looking woman came our way. She seemed as stuck up as I had been warned. I had a way of dealing with these women. Several of my clients are this type exactly. She squeezed April around the shoulders, avoiding messing up her makeup or hair. "Hello, darling. Who might this handsome gentleman be?"

I held out my hand and greeted her. "Grant Taylor. It's a pleasure to meet you. Where is Mr. Somerset?" April looked over at me and gave me a playful nudge that warned me to cool it.

"I had no idea that you would be coming with my daughter. Tell me more about you."

"Sure. Let's get a drink first. Can I get you ladies a martini?"

"You know me so well." Her mom joked. April motioned to get two. As I walked to the bar I overheard her mom saying "Did you sell your soul for that one?" She didn't know how close she was.

"We've been dating for a few months. I didn't want him to have to meet the family or my ex. That's why I didn't want to come with him."

"And this whole time you were lying. I thought you were ashamed of being single."

April laughed loudly as a queue to get me back in the conversation. Unfortunately, the bar was packed, and she would have to wait. I had several eyes looking me up and down from both men and women. Some of them were trying to see if I was a threat, and others were hoping that I was one. I wonder which one of these men were Tom. I'm sure it would be more obvious as the night went on. I got the martinis and joined April and her mother again. Her father was now standing there, looking at me with surprise.

As I approached I heard her mom whisper to him "You aren't going to believe this, honey." I gave April and her mom their drinks then held out my hand to her father. "Grant Taylor. It's a pleasure to meet you."

"The pleasure is all mine. We were certain that our daughter was in a dating drout. Little did we know she had a catch like you."

After taking several large drinks April chimed in. "Grant operates a hedge fund."

"That's true."

"It can't be." Her mom eyed me, trying to find where my cord was, as if I was a talking doll.

"Oh, but it is." I took out my business card and handed it to her and her father. I was glad I upgraded to get the nice paper on these so they looked just as classy as I was trying to emanate.

"You don't say."

"Oh, but I do." The conversation about my work continued and brought the attention away from April for a while. I could tell by the look in her eyes that she felt a lot of relief. Talking to her mom was strange. I felt like I was constantly being put to a test, like I was being measured up. April finished her drink fairly quickly.

"Maybe you could get a job as a secretary there, April."

"Okay! We should go mingle more. I'll talk to you later, mom." April grabbed my shoulder and led me around the room. She was tapped on the shoulder and jerked back. "Mrs. Middleton!"

"Hello, sweetie! We are so glad you could make it. It has really been too long. How are things going?"

"They are going well."

"And how is your writing doing?"

"I'm keeping at it. No bites yet."

"A rolling stone gathers no moss." I could tell that Mrs. Middleton already had a few. Maybe April wasn't the only one who wasn't too excited about this wedding. "Your writing is so lovely, dear, I'm sure you will get a job. I was so sad when your mom told me that you almost couldn't make it."

"Well, here I am!"

"And who might this be?"

"Grant Taylor, it's a pleasure to meet you."

"Is this your boyfriend, April."

"It sure is." You could tell by the rosiness of April's cheeks that she was boasting and gloating to Mrs. Middleton. It could have also been the alcohol.

"What a handsome fellow."

"Thank you, ma'am."

"You take good care of April. She is sublime. Simply magnificent."

"Don't I know it." April looked in my eyes and we traded a glance. She was stunning. The whole world could see it besides her.

"Tell me more about your life, dear. How are things after the accident? Did you heal properly? Do you need help?"

"I'm doing fine now, thanks." They continued talking like that for a while, catching up. I decided to excuse myself and get a drink of my own. It would be a long night for me, and I was going to enjoy it the best way I knew how.

When I joined them again Mrs. Middleton had to go talk to another family that just arrived. She gave me a hug goodbye and whispered about what a great woman April was in my ear. It was clear to me that Mrs. Middleton was nicer to April than her mother was. Perhaps that was where April's self confidence had gone. April snagged another drink and we went to a secluded table.

With my strict diet it didn't take much to get me tipsy. At this point I was fine, but another glass and I knew that I would be a little bit more cheerful and a little bit warmer. I felt like dancing with April, but I knew that this was neither the place nor the time.

There was a tinge of jealousy in my heart for her. I wished she weren't still going after this Tom guy. I knew it was hopeless, and so did she. I just didn't want her to have any feelings for him. It was crazy and stupid, especially since I was used to being the other man. Something about April just made me want to keep her safe.

12

APRIL

I need to take socializing lessons from Grant. He has mingled his way through my friends and family like no one I have seen before. He was able to successfully tame and slay the dragon that is my mother. I have never seen anyone accomplish that before, not even Tom. Not even my dad. I hoped that Mrs. Middleton wasn't upset by him being here. I wanted her to like him. I at least wanted to feel like he was welcomed. I certainly wanted him there. I wouldn't be paying him if I didn't.

Something about Grant gave me confidence. Maybe it was being seen with him, and maybe it was just the way he treated me. He had been a perfect gentleman all night, and the way he looked at me made me actually feel beautiful. All my cares and worries were disappearing.

That is, until I saw Tom. He was standing next to his fiancée laughing loudly at the front. I needed another drink. I got up to get one, but Grant insisted he grab them.

"I don't want a martini."

"That's okay. We can have armeretto sours. You'll love these."

He left to grab the drinks before I could ask how many calories were in them. When he got back I was able to finish it in a matter of seconds. It tasted like juice. We got another, and I could tell that they were starting to hit me. I kept staring at Tom, seeing him socialize with all these faces from my past. This was supposed to be me. This was going to be my wedding exactly. It was strange to see it in the position I was. It was almost like hovering over your body after you died. Tom would laugh and his soon-to-be-wife would giggle and they were having the happiest time being the two dumbest people here. Stupid happy. Stupid in love. Stupid life ruiners. "You see that turd in the suit up there? That's Tom."

"The one with the woman with the legs?"

"That one exactly."

"Okay." Grant stood up and started leaving.

"Wait!" I stage whispered. "What are you doing?"

"I'm going to go get him."

"No, are you kidding? I haven't talked to him in two years. I never want to talk to him again if I don't have to."

"Come on. You have to say something. He has to see the way you look tonight."

"It isn't worth it. I would rather die than be seen as I am now."

"I have never seen anyone as beautiful as you." When he said it that time I knew he meant it and I could feel myself falling harder. I was developing a crush on an escort. Was this an exciting new high in my life or a drastic new low? Grant slipped out of my grasp and went to go speak with him. I followed but grabbed a drink on the way.

"April." Tom sees me before I can stop Grant from saying anything. "You look... Great." I saw his fiancée eye me up and down. She linked arms with him.

"Doesn't she? I helped her pick out this dress tonight." Grant said, holding out his hand to shake. "I'm Grant Taylor."

"Oh, how do you two know each other... actually how do I know you?" Tom said, shaking the hand back. He had that dumb confused look on his face that he got when solving computer problems.

"You don't, actually. I came with April. I'm her date." I saw Tom's expression change. He kept his eyes fixed on me. "This is a lovely hotel, simply wonderful. If I ever get married, I will have to keep this place in mind." Grant turned to look at me. "Don't let me forget the name of this place, okay, honey?"

"Okay." That was all I could manage to gasp out. Tom looked great. It stung me a lot to see him. Part of my heart wasn't ready for this. When I saw his face I could feel the rush of feelings coming back through me.

"It's a pleasure to meet you." Tom stopped shaking hands. His eyes darted back and forth between the two of us. I could sense him spacing out, he was stuck in his own head now.

"And you must be the bride." Grant held his hand out to Legs and kissed her gently. "You look lovely this evening. Congrats to the both of you."

Tom began to get fidgety, his vein popping on his forehead. He was definitely jealous. "Grant, do you mind if I steal April for just a bit? Please, help yourself to some refreshments."

"Not at all." Grant kissed me on the forehead and went to the bar. I could tell my mouth was still agape. I shut it and tried to summon words to say. I wanted to yell at him for leaving me. I wanted to grab his face and kiss him hard on the mouth. I wanted to know why. I wanted to know what I did to make him not love me anymore.

"April, I have to say, you look absolutely wonderful. I almost didn't recognize you."

"Thanks."

"I'll go ahead and talk to my mom for a bit. I'll come back." Legs said, backing away awkwardly.

"So, Grant is your guy now?"

"He sure is."

"Where did you find him? He is certainly a charming fellow."

"Enchanting, isn't he?" I looked over at the bar. He was making small talk with the bartender, who was laughing hysterically at his jokes. I looked back at Tom. Boring old mean Tom. "We met at a bar. He said he couldn't stand not seeing me again. Now it's been two months."

Tom fidgeted and I could tell he was feeling just as awkward seeing me as I was seeing him. He was bothered by Grant, but couldn't say anything. Tom left first. I was never going to leave. This was all on him. "You know, I have to say, it is crazy seeing you. I almost thought you weren't going to come tonight."

"I almost didn't."

"Well, I'm glad you did. You certainly are doing well for yourself."

"I could say the same for you." I pointed at Legs. Tom glanced over too.

"Yeah, she's a great girl."

"Your mom seems like she is doing well. I missed her a lot."

"Yeah, she asks about you all the time."

"I bet that gets old. My mom does the same for you." He snickered. "My mom is actually the only reason I am here, to tell you the truth. I really didn't want to see you." The honesty was coming out, and I could feel the alcohol resting in my stomach in an uneasy way. Maybe it was the nerves. Maybe it was butterflies.

"No one can really blame you."

I was happy. Thrilled. I was so mad at Tom, but seeing him now, I'm not sure he was worth all the anger. I looked good. I was turning heads, I could tell. Maybe I wasn't as fat as I thought I was. Maybe I was worth more than Tom. I was worthy of being loved. Now I could see Tom was jealous and he didn't feel comfortable either. Me making him miserable the night before his wedding just by being there was all the boost that I needed to feel like me again. I realized we split for a good reason, whether it was cosmic fate or just restless uncertainty. I wasn't over Tom, but I was going to be.

It grew silent and I finished my drink. "You look like you're doing well, Tom."

"Thanks. You honestly look so great tonight, April."

"Yeah, thanks."

"I'm serious."

I smiled at him and tapped my empty glass. "Well, this thing isn't going to fill itself." I walked away slowly towards the bar. Grant watched me step closer and patted the seat next to him. I leaned in and whispered to him "Was he watching me leave?"

"Every step of the way. Bartender!" He shouted, playfully. "Let's get this thirsty woman some heartbreak elixir.

"It felt really shitty to see him again. There were a lot of mixed emotions."

"You're in luck. I have mixed drinks for mixed emotions." Grant joked and ordered my next drink. I swayed with the jazz music. I was fairly tipsy but I was still in my right mind. I was glad that I told Tom the truth. I was happy that he was jealous. I wanted to hurt him back for hurting me. The best thing about hurting him this way was that I wasn't doing a single thing wrong.

It felt nice to be complimented by so many people. I felt a lot less hopeless than I had a week ago. This new April kick was certainly off to a great start. I was even enjoying my time with Grant. He won over my parents and even Tom's parents. He even made me feel pretty when I wasn't halfway down to my goal weight. Grant was being a really good friend and I could tell why Alex was so close to him. I wanted to know more about his day by day life. I wondered if he really had a hedge fund. It didn't seem likely if he was an escort. And if he did, why was he an escort? There were much better ways for him to make money, or at least he didn't really have to make money.

Something about his carefree Las Vegas lifestyle really appealed to me. I wanted to be able to run away, have it so my parents stopped shaming me. I wanted to live too.

13

APRIL

This night went so much better than expected. I couldn't imagine I had summoned enough courage to talk to Tom, and even more surprised that I told him off. I wasn't the same woman anymore. I felt a bit carefree, like I was in control of my own destiny. I looked out from the windows. The night painted an illuminous portrait of the moon. The water looked like diamonds sparkling in waves, reflecting the stars and basking in the glow of the moon. So much of me wanted to jump in that ocean. Half of me wanted to confess about the lie, and the other half didn't care if I got caught. One thing was for sure, I was going to let that cool water soak into my skin before I went back to reality.

Grant sipped his last drink of the night. I had passed on having another, I was already past the point

I thought I would get to. The ice clinked on the edge of his glass as he put his pink lips on the edge. My stomach felt warm, and I didn't regret a single moment of the night. Part of me was glad I was forced to come. So much of the reservation was a fear or rejection, of being rejected again. As I looked at Grant I already reminisced about the great night we had had.

Jazz music was playing softly in the background and I swayed to it slowly. I wanted to dance. I felt like dancing. I knew I could. I could just take Grant's hand, head to the dimly lit floor and sway with him, his strong hands on my hips and his torso pressed against mine. I could smell his cologne from where I was sitting. I imagined how amazing it would smell even closer. I wanted to dance. I wanted to swim. I wanted to feel alive. I did feel alive. I wanted this feeling to last for the rest of my life, if not just the rest of this night.

"What a fantastic song." Grant said, swaying slightly with me. He put his arm around my shoulders, matching my rhythm, swaying to the bass' metronome. With the alcohol and romance in the air, I felt light, like I could float up through the ceiling. I no longer felt weighted by my pound gains or my car wreck. I didn't mind Tom, although he was staring and doing an awful job at making it subtle. I didn't feel so burdened by my debt and loans to pay off. I wasn't thinking about starting a career. I was only thinking about how wonderful the saxophone paired with the piano and bass, playing in harmony.

"It really is."

"They should play this at our wedding." Grant teased. I lightly slapped his leg and smiled. I knew he was kidding. He was either making an excellent performance, or he was toying with my emotions. He could give Meryl Streep a run for her money.

I saw my mom staring, too. She sat on the other side of the room, having to act as an invisible podium for my tipsy father and Mr. Middleton's hottest debate topic of the night. She looked unhappy. The look on her face was almost enough of an excuse to her horrible remarks at me. Almost. I could forgive her, but the emotional damage that had once pierced my soul created more problems that hadn't had to have been there. Was this dull life of hers the root of her bitter attitude?

Being able to look at her and see her that sad helped me learn to be less angry with her. I think in the future I could see where she was coming from and understand the situation better. Now I knew why she had so much hatred for Ms. Middleton. She found her to be competition. She was probably relieved when our wedding was called off, since she wouldn't have to try to get us to like her better than my other mother-in-law. My mom was very sad. I didn't like thinking about her this way, but I saw it in her eyes. At the same time, she does it to herself. This is a vicious spiral that she keeps herself in. I wasn't going to be like that anymore.

Grant ordered a glass of champagne and I turned my head to look at him. "I just wanted to enjoy this perfect moment with the perfect drink." The bartender brought over a fine crystal glass, and I ordered a second one. I could probably handle just one more drink. "A toast to a lovely couple." He remarked, clinking his glass next to my glass.

I took a sip, and the sweet taste sent a rush to my head. All the small bubbles sparked in my mouth. As I looked at the diamond encrusted waves, I felt like I was drinking the liquid star shine that reflected in the perfect water.

"I have something to tell you, Grant."

He looked at me, with a cool but somewhat concerned expression. "What is it?"

"I don't have a skin condition. I can swim just fine. I just didn't feel like surfing on a first date."

He laughed and nodded. "I thought you were going to say you had cancer or something. I'm glad to know it's the opposite." The music danced around us in the air for a moment. "In that case, we are going to have to take a dip in that water."

I looked at his eyes. They were so soft. He looked back at mine. Little by little we leaned into each other's gaze. I lost all the air in me. I closed my eyes. His lips were soft and warm, parting mine. The kiss didn't last very long, but it felt like an eternity. He tasted like champagne. I felt my heart flutter. I wanted to kiss more. When I opened my eyes, I looked around to make sure no one saw. My mother and Tom were both staring because of course they were.

It felt wrong, but also so perfect and so right. He put a hand on my knee and the shock woke me back up. It was all a lie. He was just acting. This was part of the job. This was what I paid him for. I felt disappointed. His face looked so sincere. Maybe he was sincere?

No, it couldn't have been. I wasn't going to fall for him. He had to act as the date of other women several times. He had this down to a fine art. It was all just a play and I was his stage.

Oscar for the best kiss goes to Grant and April in "Weekend at Tom's Wedding".

He grabbed my hand and kissed that too. "We better say goodbye to everyone before we go back to our room." I was still in a state of shock so all I could do was nod and follow his lead. I wasn't nearly as experienced as he was, and I wanted his charm to rub off on me. Maybe at least the alcohol would help.

We conquered our goodbyes, talking to hopefully everyone that we had to. We held hands, said what a lovely evening it was, and asked all the right questions without lingering too long. I didn't mind being the dog on his leash for social interactions. It was easier for me this way.

I felt my lips over and over with my fingers as we went to the elevators. I wanted more, but knew that I couldn't accept it.

14

GRANT

We stumbled back to the room as gracefully as we could. She made it look easy. I was having a bit more difficult time keeping it together. She had been sort of quiet in the elevators and I wondered if I had ruined the night somehow. I hoped that the kiss wasn't too far, and had I been sober I would have kept it strictly professional. She just looked so nice that evening, and she was so enchanting. Her laugh made you feel like dancing. We came as close as we could to dancing, and I'll be damned if this walk back to the room isn't a clumsy version of a waltz.

I playfully nudged her when she bumped into me. It made her smile. That was enough to tell me that she wasn't upset. Maybe she was just tired. It made no use worrying about it, but I couldn't live with myself if she were upset.

"Is everything okay?"

She looked at me with her large doe eyes. They were gorgeous. "Everything is exactly perfect."

My phone vibrated in my pocket and I wondered who would be calling me. I couldn't handle a client now. I had set all those calls to be picked up by my voicemail. Everyone knew I was out of the office. I guess that wasn't enough to keep them from ringing. I let this one go to voice mail as I put our card key in the door. Then my phone vibrated again.

I checked the screen. It was my mom. The only reason for her calling this late had to be an emergency or an accident on her part. I told April to go in the room and that I would be in there in a bit. I picked it up.

"Mom?"

"How old are you?" Her voice sounded a bit stuffy, like she had a cold.

"What?"

"How old are you?" She had to be drunk. I was preparing for the point she was going to be making. She was either calling to shame my lifestyle or my other family members. I wasn't in the mood to deal with this now, but I could tell she was fairly upset.

"Twenty-Six."

"Right. Gold star."

"Is something wrong?"

"Yes."

"What is it?"

"Abso-lutely everything."

"I need you to be more specific. Is this a mid-life crisis."

"No!" She shrieked back. "How dare you. No. Not me, but maybe your father…" Here we go. I sighed. "I mean, she's pregnant! How can someone still be fertile. How?"

"It's science."

"It's ludicrous, that's what it is! He knocked up that 32-year old-woman. How can he still have the stamina to do that? He didn't have any when we separated, I can tell you that. That well was dry to the bone."

"Can we skip those kinds of details?"

"Sorry." She hiccupped. "It just isn't fair. What does that little girl see in him?"

"I don't know."

"I'll tell you what she sees." She started answering her own question. I hardly had to be present for calls like this with my mother, she just wanted to spread her opinions on her children like fertilizer on a garden. "She sees dollar signs. You know he is older than me. He is going to croak first. Especially with the way he lives." She scoffed. "I bet he doesn't live long enough to see that brat graduate."

"That's awful, mom."

"Sorry. Sorry." She slurped something on the other side and then continued. "That baby is going to have nephews older than him. That's sick. I never thought I would have married into this kind of a family."

"Yeah, and now you divorced out of it too."

"That hurts, Grant." She sniffled.

"I know, I'm sorry, mom." Even through their marriage neither of my parents were home much. They only had themselves to blame for having a child who was an escort. I think they got tired of parenting after my first few brothers. We were all accidents, but it seemed like I was more accident than the others were.

"That really really hurts. That's a shitty thing to say."

"Sorry."

"How is your marriage going?" I tried to change the conversation.

"It's fine. Ben has to have a knee cap surgery next week and he has been complaining about his back. It makes me feel so old to date someone his age. Why couldn't he be 32. I'd even settle for 40."

"You're married and he is an appropriate age for you." That is, for her age. He was twenty years older than her. I would escort with that difference but I don't think I would ever marry with that kind of a difference. The picking pool gets slimmer the older you become.

"Yeah, well." She sniffed again. "I'm a grandma and your dad is going to be a dad again. It makes me sick."

"I'd love to chat longer about this, but I'm in the middle of something. We can talk more when I get back home."

"Of course you're busy. You're always too busy for me." She sniffled. I wasn't going to fall for her guilt trip. My conscious wasn't clumsy enough for that.

"I love you, mom."

"Fine. I love you too. Come home sometime."

I didn't like leaving my mom sad like that, but she was annoying me with her complaints and I was already annoyed by dad enough as it was. I hated hearing about that kind of stuff. He was too old to have a healthy sex life, especially with someone so young. He would be closer to death than that baby was to being an adult. My dad was never really considerate of my mom's feelings, but this wasn't really much of her business anymore. I could understand why she was upset.

I already had three other brothers. I was the baby, and so everyone thought I got off so easy. Really it meant my parents had the highest standards for me. Now there was another baby and I can't imagine the anxiety it would put on the child or how easily it would be spoiled since it was an only child. I hoped it would be an only child.

When I got back in the room April had showered and put her sweats on. She was flipping back and forth from HGTV to the Food network with a bag of chips in her lap.

"I thought you said you were on a diet."

"Yeah but I'm drunk also so," she stuck out her tongue at me. If anyone didn't need to diet, it was April. She was curved, but all of them were an excellent size. They added interest to her body. I much preferred this to all the thin women in the shows in Vegas. It was nice for a little change. She was different than them in a lot of ways. "Who was that on the phone?"

"It was my mom."

"Oh. I figured it was another…"

"Cougar?"

"Yeah."

"Well, you were still right."

"Oh." She looked over at me then back at the TV. "Complicated family."

"Definitely. Why do you think I became a hooker?"

She smiled at me and went back to watching the set on TV about remodelling a house. Outside of college I have never met anyone as anxious and semi-crazy as April. Sometimes she would talk to herself out loud. She did a really good job of drifting off into her own place It was funny to watch her chain of thoughts and what she day dreamed about. The less sad she got the more positive her dreams were. Before it seemed like she had a drive because she wanted to prove herself, but in the small amount of time that I had known her she had switched a little. It seemed like she was trying to start doing things because she wanted to and because she made them happy. She no longer seemed ashamed of me, her escort date. She was beginning to embrace the weekend and the fun we would have.

I was really hoping that now that she wanted to swim that we would. Hopefully soon. Hopefully tonight. Hopefully naked.

I sat on the bed and watched the show with her, but I wasn't really paying attention to the TV. April would point out details of certain houses, explaining that she had always dreamed of living in a place like that or with that or yadda yadda. When it was on the food network she would groan and ask me frequently if we should get food service. I had to keep turning it down, letting her know each time that I had to watch my intake and I had already gone over with the alcohol.

"Meeeee too." She laughed and finished the bags of chips. "That's why I figured why not."

"It's not like you need to stick to it that tightly, anyway."

"Yes I do." She started to look a little disappointed. "If I don't stick to it in the beginning, odds are I won't stick to it at all. But right now I'm drunk so it doesn't count."

"Right." I sorted through my bag, looking for my tooth brush.

"I'll be hot again soon."

"You're gorgeous now. You don't need to work out anymore."

"Grant. I can't be a potato forever."

"The only reason why you are saying that is because you are what you eat and you just had a bag of those."

She snorted and threw the bag at me.

"I really don't get how you don't see it. Why do you have such low self confidence?"

"My mom." She mumbled. April seemed like she was in less of a joking mood and more of a somber mood now. She was beginning to sober up.

"How does your mom make you feel bad?"

"She reminds me of the accident. She tells me about how I gained a ton of weight on it."

"That's horrible. That can't be true."

"It was 70 lbs."

I stood and blinked at her a bit. That was a lot of weight to put on. If she had gained that much and looked like this, how little had she weighed before? "Even if you are bigger than you were before, you aren't fat by any means."

"That's so sweet of you."

"But you really aren't. You just have hips and boobs." She blushed and turned it back to HGTV before the cooking was done. "Why did you switch it?"

"I don't have any more food to eat and that channel makes me so hungry."

"Then just order room service. Just because I'm not eating doesn't mean you can't."

"Please?" She looked at me with puppy dog eyes. "If I do, you have to."

It was really hard to resist. I had already gone over my diet by 563 calories, and I didn't really want to have to work all of those off when I got back home. I was having a great time, though. Maybe I could surf it off, or do some heavy dancing at the wedding. April started chanting the word "indulge" over and over, growing from quiet to fairly loud.

"Fine."

"Yay!" She picked up the phone and dialed the number. "What do you want?"

"How about a banana split?"

"Wooh! Chocolately and starchy. Just how I like it."

She told them our order, fumbling a few words when she spoke. After she hung up the receiver she crossed her arms and smiled at me.

"What?"

"Normally I'd have to recite a phone call before I made it for it to go that well." She smirked. "And I convinced pretty boy to eat tons of fat with me."

"And I convinced pretty girl to give in to her temptations."

"Whatever. You're nothing special." She said, sarcastically. I could see her cheeks become rosier each time I complimented her. It felt good to make her feel better, and it felt great to see the reaction physically. Normally people don't react that much when you compliment them, but she internalized each one.

I hope she knew I meant it with every fiber of my being. I tugged at my tie and slipped it off.

PART 3

15

APRIL

"Woah, what are you doing?" I said and Grant began to lift his shirt out of his pants. "In the bathroom."

"What? You've never seen a man shirtless before?"

I blushed.

"You know, if we go swimming, you can't exactly run away in the ocean. It's dangerous." He took his shirt off and then his undershirt. I looked away. When I looked back he was laying in the bed with only his boxers and a hotel robe on.

"What are you doing?"

"Laying down."

"No way. You're going to sleep on the couch."

"No I'm not."

"It's part of the deal."

"No, I just said I won't be sleeping with you. I never said I wouldn't be sharing a bed sleeping with you."

"You have to."

"It's too uncomfortable."

"It's perfectly comfortable. You haven't even sat on it, how would you know?"

"You haven't sat on it either." He was right, but I was starting to become impatient. "You wouldn't know if it's comfy or not. And if it's that comfy, why don't you sleep on it?"

"My invite, my rules."

He chuckled, rolling his eyes. "Well you are just going to have to deal with this. I'm not going to break my back just because you don't want to share." He got up and went to the bathroom. "I still have to shower. You can get used to the idea while I am gone."

The ice cream was delivered and I stress ate. The more food I put in my body, the more I could feel myself becoming sober. If I hadn't gotten to be better friends with him I probably would have offered him the bed instead of the couch. I felt comfortable enough with him now, though, to demand he be the bigger man. It's funny how quickly you can be acquainted to someone when put in high stress situations with plenty of booze. Especially when you are both about the same amount of comfortable. Actually, he seemed more used to this than me. He could dance his way through social groups like a ballerina. I was going to have to read his book on how to be a charming person without having sex with them.

I finished all the ice cream. He took incredibly long showers. I wondered if maybe he had more products than me or if he needed time to settle. I heard the water turn off so I tucked myself under the covers, hoping that if I couldn't argue his way out of sleeping on the bed. I could hog the bed to a point where he didn't want to sleep on it. The door began to open. I squeezed my eyes shut and did my best drunk impression of a sleeping person.

"Are you going to scoot over, or am I going to have to make you?" I peeked out of one of my eyes. He started to take off his robe, wearing nothing but his boxer briefs. Each of his abs were like little mountains on his stomach. It took all my effort not to stare. I did an awful job. He slid into the bed, nudging me onto one side as he did.

"Separate blankets." I said, hoping that the layers would give us some distance. He respected my request, letting out a sigh and rolling his eyes a bit.

I could see by the smirk on his face that I had assumed right. He loved to shock me. I don't know if it made me blush every time he did, but my face got hot. I wondered how he knew. What part of me was giving away my inner thoughts? "Why do you keep surprising me?"

"Your face gets rosy and you babble. You just speak your mind. It's like you lose control of your tongue. And who doesn't like to have their body marveled?"

"Me."

He looked at me, some sorrow in his eyes. I could tell my self pity was starting to annoy him. He had told me I was beautiful enough times for me to get annoyed by that even. We both said nothing. Looking in his eyes I could see the sharp details in the pools of brown. He looked caring. He looked trustworthy. He looked like he cost a million dollars, which I didn't have.

I could still feel his body through the sheets we had between us. All my hopes for a fun sleepover with him were dashed out of my head. I had lived with a gay male for so long that I forgot how to interact with a straight one. This wasn't like a best friend sleepover, and that made it difficult for me to know how to act. I wanted to play his game. I wanted to shock him back. I wanted to know what that power felt like.

"I didn't save any ice cream for you. You shouldn't have showered so long." I sassed.

"Good. I didn't want any."

Damn. This was going to be harder than it seemed.

He started to lean in, and I scooted back a little. I wanted to lean in too, though. So badly. I wanted to feel those lips again. I hate how badly I wanted to be with him. I hate that he knew that. I hate that I couldn't tell if he was taking advantage of my wallet or my heart. There was no way that I could kiss him. I couldn't kiss him this weekend, at least.

"What?" He opened his eyes. I surprised him this time, not giving in.

"We can't."

"Why not?"

I didn't answer. I was afraid that if I did I would offend him. I didn't know how to respond. His brown eyes pierced through mine. I wanted to kiss him. I felt guilty for giving in and guiltier for not giving in. I couldn't afford him enough already, and if this was a clever Vegas trick, I would be on the streets in no time.

I didn't want to think of the future anymore. All that had given me is worry and a false sense of insecurity. Things always work out, and if they didn't, I could cross that bridge when I got to it. I needed to shock him back, to put him in his place. He still looked at me, but had eased away a bit.

I repeated myself.

"We just can't."

I didn't want to say that I couldn't afford him. I didn't want to say that I never thought I would go this far with a prostitute. I didn't want to say anything. And I didn't have to. He seemed to read my mind, his eyes seeing my thoughts. Grant leaned in, kissing me on the mouth anyway, not caring about what that I thought.

And I stopped thinking when he did that. I didn't feel anything but the rush of blood that his mouth was giving me. I felt light. His lips were caressing mine sweetly. I had resisted enough tonight, I decided to indulge myself. I kissed him back, hard. Our lips parted and we kept kissing and kissing, long and soft, then quickly and hard. Our tongues would dance with each other, licking the inside of our mouths. He put his hand on my cheek. It was like a pillow and released a world of butterflies into my stomach. I reached back, my hand on his head too, all the while pressing my lips onto his.

I couldn't think anymore. I could only feel. My primitive being was taking over, and I felt hot. I wanted him. I combed my fingers through his hair. It was still a little wet, but soft and silky in the dry parts. It felt like a feather dancing across my fingers. I wanted to giggle. I resisted that urge, keeping my mouth occupied with his.

We kissed for a long time. We kissed hard. I was justifying this to myself in my head, trying to silence my dizzying thoughts. He never said a kiss would cost me anything. And he started it. This was all his doing. It could be off the books if it was out of his own control, right?

He moved his hand down, slowly, passing over my neck and then shoulder, to where it was under the covers on my arm. It was beneath the sheet that separated us. He rested it on my waist, putting the other hand back up behind my neck again. I wondered if he could feel my pulse, beating against his hand.

I started to move my hand too, mimicking him. It went down to his neck, to his shoulders, and it stopped as I placed it over his peck. It was firm and soft. His skin was gentle but firm underneath. His muscles rippled. I moved it down, stopping on his side.

My head tore back. I looked in his eyes. I had gone this far without asking. I wanted to ask. I wanted to say "what are we doing?" but I couldn't, because I knew very well. His eyes were so dreamy. He didn't think anything of my pulling back. He just leaned forward again, waiting for me to kiss him back. And I did. And with that his hand moved up my shirt.

I wanted to suck in my stomach, but now it was too late to do that. He rested his palm on the curve of my waist, petting me back and forth. Everything in me felt alive. His fingers were rubbing my back sweetly, reassuring me that this was fine. It was fine. I felt fine. I felt great. I felt wonderful, like this mattress was a cloud and we were floating high above that dumb party and dumb rent and other fees. We were carelessly sailing the sky, just kissing.

It felt right here with him. I felt cared for. I felt the outline of his penis on the sheet between us. I tossed it up. Every part of me fell into a million pieces as he touched me, trailing his hand up to my bra. I pulled him in tighter, kissing his neck slowly. He smelled like a candle I had had months ago. He smelled like summer. My lips moved back to his mouth as he reached behind and unhooked my bra. I was surprised by how quickly he unfastened it. He liked surprising me. He liked surprises.

I took this opportunity to shock him back. I put my leg on him, flipping into a straddling position. His hands rested on my waist. I could feel him hard beneath me. I noticed my breathing was uneven. I kissed him on the mouth again slowly. His hands pushed up on my shirt until it was off. I pulled back a little. It had been so long that all these sensations felt so new to me. His lips met mine again, slowing even more. I leaned down on him, my hands behind his head, twisting in his hair.

His palms curled up my waist back up to the bra. He took it off slowly, kissing my arms as he pulled it down them. I gasped. He loved it, kissing hard, trailing back up to my shoulder, my neck, my mouth.

His hands curled around my thighs, then trailed up my back just as slowly as the kisses had trailed to my mouth. I could feel goose bumps raise up on my arms. A chill was sent through my back. He smiled under my kiss and traced his fingers to my breasts, gently grabbing them.

Everything felt so sensitive. My heart was beating out of my chest. I wondered if he could feel it beneath his hand, tapping out a message in Morse code. It was screaming for him to take me. It was screaming his name. It was screaming, and all I could do was let muffled gasps escape under our kisses. He was still smiling. His fingers squeezed gently, making me make more noise.

He bit my lip gently. His tongue dipped into my mouth then out, licked my lips. He kissed my cheek, and I could feel it was hot from my blushing that he loved so much. He kissed my neck. Did I smell like summer too? He kissed my shoulder. Then moved his mouth down, making a trail of kissing to my chest, sending a jolt to my head each kiss he gave.

My hips twisted. He let out a small breath. He was hot too. I pulled back, kissing him on the mouth. My hands released his hair and grabbed at his boxer seams. I couldn't resist him anymore.

I realized what I was doing and stopped myself. He had to make the advances. I wanted him to do it. And as if he could read my mind, he did, shoving an index finger down in between my pants and my panties. He grabbed at the seam of my pants with both hands, now. Tugging them down little by little.

I tore down on his boxers. I felt his penis beneath me. He drew back, opening his eyes up at me. "Your turn."

He didn't have to say it twice. I rolled onto my back, where he worked quickly, pulling down my pant and then my panties. I kicked them off. His hands came back, one resting on my boob, and the other on my hips, thumb petting back and forth on my pelvis. He pulled his head back and smiled at me.

"You're beautiful."

I couldn't respond. I had too much adrenaline rushing through my body. I didn't know how to respond. He didn't wait for me to say anything. He kissed me again, this time trailing from my mouth down to my neck, down my cleavage, down to my stomach, and then he worked his way to my hips, kissing the side before he started licking me. I sighed. His hands pushed my legs, bending the knees up and apart, far enough to keep his body in as he started to suck on my clit.

His hands pet my thighs as he did this. I sighed. I kept sighing, gasping, and letting out little moans. He pushed into me, taking me by surprise. I put my hands on his head and he pulled it up. He had a boyish grin on his face. He kissed my body back up, slowly, until he stopped at my neck.

"Kiss me." I sighed. I didn't care where his mouth had been. I didn't care about anything but him and I. He did as I said, kissing me gently. He drew back and stopped. I almost asked what was wrong, but then I saw him slide the condom on.

Okay. So this was all real. And it was all happening. Okay. Good. Great. I felt a bit embarrassed as I lay there, naked. No one had seen me naked at this size. Had I known that I would have gone this far, I would have done more maintenance and probably ran a few miles today. It was too late to care about that now. His smile was reassuring though, as he scooted back up and slid inside me.

His body beat against mine, very slowly and gently. I kissed his mouth, again and again. My legs curled around and I rested my hands on his back. He kissed me back, then moved to my neck, kissing and breathing heavily. He was sweet and gentle. Too gentle. I kissed him, turning my body so we were side by side and then I was on top.

I brought my head back. I saw he was blushing now too. I bounced on him, feeling powerful. I could see him, waiting for me to kiss him. I did, but it wasn't on the mouth. I kissed his neck. I humped faster and harder than he had been. I felt electricity building up in my body. I heard my self sighing and I could hear him breathing just as heavily as me, if not harder.

I climaxed, blood rushing through my body. He was still going, so I kept going. I felt all my stress run out of my body, I was relaxed. He grabbed me and flipped me back so that I was on bottom, and he was on top.

This time he didn't kiss me either. He leaned over me, looking me in the eyes. They were so gentle. He pounded and pounded until he winced and shook. He pulled out and rolled over, panting like a dog.

"Wow." He gasped, checking the clock. It was late. Very late. I got up to go to the bathroom, still a little wobbly and weak in the knees. I was stone cold sober now. I felt alive. I splashed some water on my face and went through my routine, brushing my hair and teeth.

If I was going to pay for that, it was worth the money. I would have to see if he took layaway. I cleaned my face and threw a baggy shirt on. He was laying on the bed, body turned towards me. He was sweaty and above the covers, his boxers were back on.

"Do you have any water?" He asked me. I reached into the mini fridge and gave him one. He drank it quickly, emptying almost half of it. I laid down next to him and asked if he wanted to watch a show.

"Sure. I might fall asleep, though. That took a lot out of me."

"Yeah, me too." I lied. I had never been more awake in my life. I flipped the TV on and he turned the lights out. I pondered moving to the couch, but I figured there was no point in that anymore. The deed was done. He was asleep in a matter of minutes and I was awake, staring past the infomercials before me, mind swimming with thoughts. It took a few hours before I fell asleep.

16

GRANT

When I woke up I noticed drool on my pillow. I hadn't drooled since I was a kid. April wasn't next to me anymore. I flipped the pillow over and rested my head back, thinking about the night before. She was just as hot as I imagined, and even hotter underneath all those clothes with her hair all messed up. Thinking about her made me want her to be in bed next to me, ready for a second round.

Of course, she wasn't there, though. I decided to take a cold shower. I had sweat enough that I was starting to get a bit stinky, so I popped in the shower. I couldn't stop thinking about her. Her lips were like a little bow, perched on her face. Even the shower didn't help take my mind off of it. Switching to cold water, I rinsed out my hair and tried to plan for the day.

If we had time, we would have to go enjoy the water. The shower was hardly enough to satisfy my thirst, my craving. I needed the ocean like the fish did. When I got back in the room I could hear the waves lapping onto the beach. April was out there, two coffees on the table.

Sneaking over, I kissed her on the top of the head and took one of the coffees.

"Thanks. After this and last night, I can't see how you're still single."

She ignored my flirtation. "I didn't know how you took it, so I brought up some cream and sugar packets too."

"I take it black. Or with a little bit of ice cream." I smiled at her again. She didn't smile back. I saw her coffee looked like a mug of milk with a hint of coffee in it. "How are you feeling today?"

"A little hung over, but okay."

We both sat there for a while, taking in the view. "Do you think there will be time to swim? We should go when we get a chance."

"I don't know if we will, between the party and every other thing that has to happen in between." I was disappointed, but I understood.

"I figured. I'll just come back out here sometime and surf. I used to be really big into surfing. I still am, actually, but college gave me a lot more free time. Especially since I was directly on a beach. Sometimes my escorts will let me surf, a few even go with me, but most of the time they want to go to paradise without actually getting a feel for it." I felt so natural around her that I forgot not to talk about previous jobs. I just wanted to talk about everything with her. Talking about my work was starting off on the wrong foot. I looked at her eyes. She didn't seem bothered. She was blushing, again, however. She reached into her bag, and pulled out an envelope and handed it to me.

My stomach turned. "What's this?" I could guess what it was. I was worried that she would have felt like this. What happened last night had nothing to do with her needing me here, what had happened was between us. I thought we had a connection. I opened the envelope. There were four crisp one hundred dollars bills that I know she had to go to the bank for. I looked back at her. She smiled, and I wanted to forgive her. I couldn't. Now I knew what she had thought of me that whole time.

"Is this a joke?" I was stunned. Normally that was her job. The look on her face was confusion. I threw the envelope back on the table and picked up my coffee, scolding hot. I drank it anyway. She still wasn't talking. I don't think she knew what to say. "Wham-Bam-Thank-You-Sir" wasn't a great rhyme, so I am sure she was speechless on how to treat a prostitute like me.

"Are you mad?"

"Hell yes I'm mad. I'm livid."

"Why? If someone handed me that I would be thrilled." She brushed her hair out of her face and looked out to the ocean. I could tell she was trying to stay calm. She had had a glow around her until I started yelling. Now she looked frustrated, but she stayed calm still, keeping her eyes on the water.

"Money has nothing to do with what happened between us." I said each word like they ended with a period. "You don't need to think much of me, I don't work for Google or anything, but you can at least treat me like a human being, and not some commodity to buy."

I realized the irony in my statement as I said it. I was exactly that. I sold myself to women for money. The whole reason I took this job wasn't even for the money. It was for the thrill of making someone else pleased. It was so different from home. My parents were both always measuring me up to other people and kids. Being an escort was one of the few escapes I had where someone could be thrilled by the sight of me and want me to visit again and again.

"Woah, I don't care if you work for Google, I don't care if you're an escort or not. I just - "

"Isn't that what this whole thing is? You want to get hot, which you already are. That piece of shit just didn't know what he had and so he didn't treat you like a person. You want to find a great date, say he is perfect for you and make me do this dance and song for your parents and friends and they are super impressed. They all see how happy you are doing, but not really and for what? So you can show up at your perfect ex-fiancee's wedding, with someone strapped to you just to prove to everyone that you could turn out fine?"

I felt like an ass as I said it. Words were just pouring out of my mouth. I saw the hurt look in her eyes. I wanted to help, but she hurt me first.

"Besides, if you really wanted to buy me, you couldn't afford me. I charge ten times that, sometimes more. Keep your money. You need it more than I do."

That pushed it over. I didn't care how much I hated myself at that point because some small part of me knew that it needed to be said. The other old ladies and billion-millionaires knew that I was their toy. They took me places, and I did the same song and dance for them. But with them it was all a charade. With her it was real. It felt real. If it weren't, I would have pulled out more tricks last night, believe me. I don't need to keep it simple, I just chose to. I didn't want our first time to be a mockery of sex. I wanted her to feel like she was wanted back. Apparently I did a shitty job at it.

I finished my coffee and slammed down the mug. I wanted to leave. I wished I had never met her. Not like this. This was not how it was suppose to go. We were supposed to be laughing and naked, still on the bed. We should have had morning sex, the only thing better than the first time. It's so playful and fun. Instead we were doing business over coffee. I wanted April to be the exception. I didn't know how to feel. I didn't know how to react. All that came out was my anger and disappointment.

I had never acted like this before. Normally when I am bothered by something I can take it in calm strides. I don't know what was different this time. I felt like a child throwing a fit. My mind was going in circles. I was upset with her but I also wanted to help her at the same time. I didn't want to be mad. I didn't want to stay mad. I didn't want to feel like an object to her, though. I thought that it was clear that what we were doing was off the books. Apparently not. I should start saying "Off the record" to her. That would be annoying. That would be dumb.

I noticed I was pacing in the room. I went back and forth between the bed and the porch. I didn't know what to say. I wanted to turn back time to before the fight. I wanted to turn back time to before we started flirting back and forth. I hoped she wasn't just acting back. I certainly wasn't acting around her.

I left her like that, silent and confused. I went into the room and got dressed. I only had nice clothes, but I didn't feel like wearing them now. I felt like going down to the lobby in pajamas and just kicking back. I felt like doing a couple laps from here to Asia to blow off steam.

This was the first time I felt like this. I hadn't felt used before. Not that she had used me. I don't really know what was making me so mad, but I was hoping this wedding could get over quickly. The faster I was out of here, the faster I could regain my sensibility. I wanted to swim. I wanted to run. I wanted to do something to blow off this steam. I didn't have the right clothes or time for any of these apparently, so I decided maybe drinking was my best option. Lucky for me, I get all the drinks I need on the house. Apparently I'm worth that much here.

"I'm going down to the lobby." I shouted at her.

She didn't know what to say or how to respond. I could tell I shocked her, but not in the way I wanted to. It was all unpleasant. I just grabbed the clothes that were on top of the rest and threw them on. I left the room, shoes in hand. I put them on in the elevator.

17

APRIL

I was silent. My mind ran in circles and my mouth fell open. Did that just happen? All I could do was stare at the door he just slammed. Did that really just happen? I didn't know what to do or say. I was speechless. How did that just happen? I counted in my head when he said it. Four thousand dollars for one night? That was ridiculous. I couldn't believe that. What was happening? What was happening right now?

I felt a little bad for assuming that he was just doing what he was doing for money, but at the same time, we never established there was anything outside of that. I started to cry a little. This weekend had been an emotional roller coaster. What goes up must come down, I just didn't know why it had to be a plummeting crash when I was only just experiencing life above sea level.

The shouting had hurt my head. I took a couple ibuprofens with my coffee and finished the cup. I wasn't sure what my next move should be. It was early in the day, but there was already so much that had happened and much more for me to do.

I was surprised that he just stormed out. That seemed out of character for him. He had been so calm and cool the whole time I knew him. I never thought he was capable of blowing up like that. I didn't know what he was doing in the lobby, and I didn't care to see him yet. I was upset. I didn't do anything wrong. I just wanted to make sure that I wasn't taking his acts the wrong way.

I wiped my eyes and took a long long shower. I was right about him having more products than me, and they were the really really nice stuff. I hadn't even heard of some of these brands. I was sure that they were made with Oprah's tears. I decided to use some of them. He could more than afford it, if he made that much money. No wonder he was so clean. I was glad he charged that much. If I had gotten someone that had actually only charged $400 I might have been skinned or gotten mange.

My hair felt so soft after I used his shampoo. I smelled vaguely like colognes. My skin had never been fresher. I was going to have to steal some of this and put it in a travel container. If he was going to accuse me of using him, I might as well actually use him.

When I got out I rapped myself in the robe he had worn the night before and called Travis. He better have a great explanation for this. He didn't answer the first time. I dialed again, and he picked up on the first ring. "Hey, I'm at the gym. Is everything okay?"

"Four thousand dollars?"

"Oh shit."

"Four. Thousand!?"

"So you know, then?"

"Of course I know. When were you planning on telling me? What did you have to do to get this kind of a deal, anyway? Sell your soul? Did you sell mine?"

"Girl. Chill. I was doing you a favor. You are broke as a joke."

"But he doesn't need to know that! He is just there for the weekend for you."

"Yeah, but…"

"Oh no."

I took a deep sigh. I was in it now. I hadn't realized how strong my feelings for him were until I was scared that he was no longer a possibility to me.

"You have feelings for him, don't you?"

"Yeah. I guess."

"Well you are going to have to do some crazy magic, because I can't afford to buy him for you every night of the week."

"Well… Actually…" I was quiet for a moment.

"Go on."

"Last night we kind of…"

"Kissed?"

"Yes.

"So?"

"And there was more." My voice squeaked at the end.

"Uhh.. How much more are we talking?"

"We are talking, like, all the way."

"Like… You went all the way all the way?"

"Yeah."

"Like not just a hug or something, but him penetrating inside of you all the way?"

"Gross." There was never an excuse to use the word penetration, even if it was in an appropriate or correct usage. "But yeah. And this morning just made it worse."

"Why? Did you double dip? Is he sending a ransom to your family for the dirty cash?"

"No. We were at breakfast, and I gave him the money because I figured, well, I don't know. I didn't want him to think he wasn't getting paid."

"Sure, yeah. I get that." He was breathing heavy in the background. I could tell he was starting to run again.

"But then he got super pissed. He slammed his coffee on the table and started yelling about how I'm a horrible person and how last night had nothing to do with money, and then he just stormed out and he has been in the lobby for god knows how long now."

He stopped breathing heavy. I could tell he stopped again. "So…"

"So?"

"So he has feelings back?"

"I… I guess…."

"Weird."

"Yeah." I picked some of the paint off of one of my fingers. "What do I do?"

"I don't know, I have never had to deal with that kind of drama. Prostitutes are all news to me."

"You think I have experience?" I scoffed.

"More than I do. As of now."

"Shut up."

"Sorry." He started jogging again. His speech was becoming quick.

"So you see my dilemma."

"Girl, I would help you if I knew how, but your situation was already fucked before you even got the party invite."

I sighed. "Yeah, you're telling me."

"If you want my honest opinion, I'd say ask him how he really feels. It's not your fault that you thought a prostitute might have been sleeping with you for money."

I chuckled. Travis was the best at making me laugh. He knew that too, so he pushed harder.

"And how would anyone believe that he would want to touch someone as hideous as you?"

"I know. I get confused with the sea monsters so often I have my own fan page dedicated to the search for me."

He laughed too. "I have had people come to our house and ask me for pictures or evidence of life in your natural habitat."

"Yeah, a lot of people do the same for you." We both sighed.

"I'll have a ton of wine waiting for you when you get back. I have to go. Keep me updated."

"Okay. Just know I hate you forever for lying."

"Yeah, you'll get over it."

The line clicked. He was right. I would get over it. It wasn't close to the worst thing that had happened to me the past year. Sadly, it was actually one of the nicer things anyone had done for me in a while. I didn't have a clue what to do. The engagement party was tonight, and my paid-date was mad at me for paying for him, my mom would kill me if I didn't show and ridicule me if I were alone. I didn't want to have to deal with any of this anymore.

Maybe I was wrong to come here. Did I really care that much about my parents approval? I was an adult now. I can make all my own decisions. I should have just stood up for myself. My mom could have dealt with me not coming here. Why would she want me to come? Having been left before, she should know how bad it hurts to see Tom. It makes it even worse that he is with another person, and he is having the time of his life.

I had had enough. I didn't care what my parents would say, I'd take them yelling at me. I grabbed a towel and put on my swim suit. If I was going to have to be held hostage here in Santa Barbra, then I was going to swim. I wiped both of my cheeks to get rid of the tears and put on the suit I had packed. I still felt weird wearing a one piece, but I had felt a little self esteem boost from last night. I wondered if I was really as good looking as everyone had said. I would have to see the reaction tonight when I didn't choose the skimpiest dress I owned.

I put on some of the sun screen. It smelled like a pina colada and I wanted one so bad. I was avoiding going downstairs still. It was probably best to let Grant deal with his anger in his own way and just come back upstairs when he blew off some steam. I called room service again. They were going to have my face and room number memorized. I put an order for two pina coladas in, extra strong.

While I waited, I paced the room. Tonight was the engagement. Tonight. I had to do so much in so little time. Swimming was not realistic. I didn't care. I didn't want to think about all the things I had to do to get ready. I didn't want to think about having to apologize to Grant. I was in the wrong for giving him the money, but at the same time this was the most intense and confusing thing that has ever happened to me.

I drank the drinks when they came up and watched some more TV. I had to work up the courage to walk through the lobby. It was going to take all my effort and mental capacity to stay calm and look like I had the perfect life that I had painted for everyone last night. The alcohol helped give me that extra push I needed. I put normal clothes on over my swim suit, just in case I needed to do not fun things instead of not caring. I went out of the room and walked past the elevator and to the stairs. I knew I was going to regret this the next day. I started walking down the steps, hoping this would be a good enough work out for the month.

18

GRANT

I was mad. Mostly at myself. I had never yelled at a client before, and maybe that is because I didn't think of April as one. I walked to the bar, jacket held tight in my hands. The staff greeted me with a smile and I tossed the card down.

"Mimosa, please. Keep them coming."

This is what breakfast looks like when your day needs an extra kick to keep up with you.

The more I thought about it, the madder I became at myself. It wasn't April's fault. She didn't know. If I had been in her situation I probably would have been more confused than ever. She didn't deserve to get yelled at. I did. I made it unprofessional, and I fell for my client. I had sworn before that that would never happen. I had never expected to have a woman like April, though.

There had to be some way that I could patch this up. I downed the mimosa and rested my head in my hands.

"Tough morning?" One of the bartenders asked. He was shinning a glass with a rag, just like the stereotypical image that every TV show and movie used. I had to laugh.

"I couldn't begin to explain it even if I wanted to."

He nodded back at me. An order on the phone came and he started to make two pina coladas. They looked so nice, though it was a bit early in the day. I budgeted more calories in my diet for trips, so it wasn't the worst idea, just a bad one.

"I'll have one of those, too."

The bartender smiled and sent me one over. It was thick and luscious, served in a pineapple. I raised my glass to him and drank. It woke up the part of my mind that was still asleep.

"I don't know what's going on, so maybe this doesn't apply, but I don't think you should let your vacation here be spoiled. It's so lovely outside and there is so much to enjoy. When you remember this place, are you going to want to remember the bad times or all the good?"

Bartenders have a way of looking into your soul and seeing your desires and fears. He was right about not spoiling the vacation. Even if it was ruined between April and I, I could still enjoy the weather and these drinks. "That's excellent advice." I drank more of the pineapple. "Normally, I'm the one who fixes problems for a living. It's nice to have someone else for a change."

"Are you a doctor?" He said. "Like, a therapist or something?"

"Something like that." Some people considered sex therapy. Those people were called sex addicts, and they were some of my best clients. I checked my watch. It was eleven. There was still enough time to enjoy the day.

Finishing the pina coladas, I ordered another mimosa. The champagne bubbles and orange juice were just what I needed. I turned in my chair, surveying the room. I saw some people getting breakfast from the party last night. I hadn't recognized most of them, I only talked to the people that April had known. Entering the lobby as I looked was Tom. I avoided eye contact. If there was one thing that this morning did not need heaped onto it, it was an interaction with that guy.

"Hey," I said to the bartender. "You see that guy over there in the brown button up?" The bartender nodded. "What is he doing?"

"Well, he is looking around. Okay, he is looking at you. He is staring at you. He is starting to walk over here."

"Shit." I raised my glass to him. "Good luck to both of us, then." I downed the drink and felt a hand on my left shoulder.

"Hey, buddy."

"Oh, hey Tom. How are things going today?"

His eyes were bloodshot and heavy with baggage. "Great."

"Ready for today's adventures?"

"As ready as I'll ever be." He ordered a rum and coke. I decided he might have had a worse start to this morning than I had. "How does a man like yourself get away with a weekend from work?"

"Great employees."

Tom smiled weakly back at me. "What do you do, if you don't mind me asking?"

"I own a hedge fund."

He let out a soft whistle. "How did you get that gig? Help from your parents?" I could see doubt in his eyes. I took out my wallet, fishing for a business card.

"I started as a day trader and worked my way up. I am pretty good with it, and so I figured I would let other people get a chance to practice their own skills." I handed the card to it, and he held it from the corners like a photograph or item for a museum. I wondered if I should have waited for him to put gloves on first.

He slid the card into his pocket. "So you're good with finances then?"

"It's my job." That part was true.

"I have to be honest, I'm not having the best luck." I looked around at the lavish hotel. This wedding was a huge expense. His parents must have been paying for it. I could imagine them both happily writing out a big check for their turd of a son for getting married. "I don't actually know how I am going to get a house after all this." He swirled his finger in the air. A man like him, I would have assumed he already had a house.

"I just thought that anyone who worked for Google would be given a crown and a thrown in a palace somewhere." I kid back.

He chuckled and took a drink. "You would think so. Google is actually…" he stopped talking. He shook his head and took several large gulps.

"Are they suffering?"

"Far from it. I just might be. They don't seem to be too thrilled with me." He shrugged. "I don't know why I'm telling you all of this. He looked up at me and then back down at his drink. He picked at his fingers. He and April had the same nervous habit.

"I have a trustworthy face."

"That must be it."

"Sorry to hear about your situation."

He waved his hand as he finished the last of his drink. "Don't worry about it. Let's not talk about it. How are things with April?"

"Oh, fantastic. I was actually looking at the wedding packages here." I wasn't the type of person who normally kicked someone when he was down, but I wanted to do this for her. It would be a nice way of saying I'm sorry and for him to feel miserable for giving up a great girl. He cringed a little when I said the word wedding. I wasn't sure if they were harsh feelings towards marriage or towards me being with his ex. "She is doing really well. She has had several articles published and she is working on a series right now for the Huffington Post."

"You're kidding."

"I wish. Then I would have more time with her." He nodded at me, eyes wide with surprise.

"Yeah, they still have to see whether they want to finish this project or move on to a new one. This one might be losing its edge, according to April, but I wouldn't know. It's top secret so I haven't read it. She always wants my opinions on writing, too, so this is a little hard for me."

His jaw was clenching and unclenching. He ordered another drink. This one was without the mixer.

"The strangest part is how humble she is about it. I am so proud of her. I want to carry her through every room like a prize that I've won. I can't believe she likes someone as boring as a day trader."

"Sounds like it's going well, then."

"It's going better than ever. You're going to have to keep this between you and me, but she could be the one. I don't think this wedding place is for us, but when I find the right one, that's when I'll have to pop the question."

"Relationship is going well, then?"

"I have never met anyone that I am more in sync with than April. She is so kind and gentle and has this adorable quirky way of doing everything. She is funny and sweet and has this energy about her." The bartender asked me if I would like another drink. I declined. I shouldn't have yelled at her. Maybe I wouldn't have if I wasn't nursing a small headache. I didn't need anymore to drink. "Her skin is so soft and her smile. Her smile is the brightest thing in the room." I looked over at Tom and he looked back, blank expression on his face. "Sorry. I forgot who I was talking to."

"It's fine. She really is something."

I could tell by the way he said it he was conflicted. This was April's dream, to get Tom back. I didn't want to get in the way of making her happy. I didn't want him to get in the way of me being happy, either. All the things I had said about April were true, and I did really feel that way. I wasn't ready to get married, by any means, but she is the type of person that I imagined a wedding with as soon as I met her. I was crushing hard. If the bartender wanted me to have a good time, I was going to have a good time. I nodded back at him. "How about this girl of yours? Wife material, apparently."

He finished his second drink and looked at me. "Very much so. She's something else."

"She is beautiful." I didn't feel bad for rubbing it in his face, but I could tell that he was starting to. "You two seemed really happy together last night."

"I wish it was like that every night." He seemed tired still. I wondered if they had fought too.

"Weddings can be stressful. I'm sure you two will spring back when this is all over." I ordered a drink of water. It was cool and soothed my throat. I had been doing an awful lot of drinking and not a lot of hydrating. It's what my body had needed. I felt relief as soon as I took a drink. My hangover began to subside and I felt much better.

Tom ordered another drink. He had time until the party tonight, so hopefully he would sober up by then. He swayed in his chair. I could see what he and April had in common, but I could also see how different they were.

"What was April like when you guys were in college?"

He laughed.

"Between you and me, high strung. Type A personality. She had everything figured out and would finish her projects weeks in advance. She didn't really have too many friends, at least not after a while. We kind of became hermits and hung out mostly with each other."

"Ah. Did you know Travis?"

His eyes perked up. "I love Travis."

"Travis is the reason why we met. I'm actually from Las Vegas."

"I wondered why your card said that."

"Yeah. April and I sort of bumped heads at first, but the more I see her the more I love her." I couldn't believe I said those words. It had been too little of time to tell if I actually loved her, or so I thought. I didn't know much about love. I had never been in love before. What I felt for April, though, was a stronger crush than any I have had on any other woman.

"Well, I'm glad she found someone as great as you. Now maybe my parents will stop making puppy dog eyes at me and bringing her up in front of Chelsea. It's getting obnoxious. They really liked her and never really let her go."

April peered into the room, two empty glasses in her hands. She was swaying a little as she walked, in a very cat like manner. She walked over to us and fixed her hair countless times before she reached the bar. She looked like her heart had dropped. When she noticed me looking at her she raised her nose in the air. She stuck the two drinks down on the counter.

"Hey, you." I said, grabbing her waist and pulling her towards me. She smelled like coconut. I could see her swim suit straps underneath the dress she was wearing. She smiled and looked less tense when I grabbed her, so I kissed her on the cheek too. She blushed and straightened her dress.

"Hello, Tom."

"You look nice today, April." She had had her hair up in a messy bun and was makeup less but I agreed with him whole-heartedly. She had a natural beauty about her.

"Thank you, Tom." She kissed me back and I could smell the pina coladas on her breath. I ordered her a glass of water, making sure that she had the same relief I did. I put the little card the manager had given me back in my pocket. I'm sure we could make use of it later tonight.

"I was just telling Tom here about your work with the Huffington Post." Her eyebrows raised up. I knew she was a bad actress, so I did the talking. "I told him about how it was secret, though. Seriously, Tom, I haven't even read any of it."

"I'm sure it will be great." Tom looked between me and April. Instead of anger or jealously I saw something else in his eyes. He looked relieved. It seemed that he no longer actually wanted April. I wondered if there was something about her that made him call off the wedding, something that I hadn't noticed yet. In my eyes she was perfect.

After seeing April, I no longer felt mad at her. I don't know if she still only thought of me as an escort, but I saw that she had felt bad for it before and would stop treating me like one. That was all I asked. If she didn't want to be with me, that was fine, but I didn't want to be led around and led on. It would hurt much worse with her than the others. I didn't mind being a toy to the others, but with her I wanted to be a person.

I wanted her to know that I wasn't mad anymore. I didn't have harsh feelings about this morning towards her, but it did sting. I couldn't tell if she thought I was acting or not. I liked it that way. That way she made the choice for how our relationship was going to continue forward.

"I should probably be going." I could tell Tom had felt uncomfortable around April, and April felt the same way back. It would be strange to go to your ex's wedding. Especially when they weren't on mutual terms. Tom put a tip on the counter for the bar keeper. "Thanks for talking to me, Grant. I'll be seeing you, April."

"Bye, Tom." When he left he did look over his shoulder at her, twice. Both times he had been struck with a confused expression. I could see him teetering back and forth between wanting her and wanting nothing to do with her. I didn't mind. The more envious he was, the more my job was completed.

April sat where he was sitting at the bar. She was silent and not making eye contact with me. I couldn't read her right now.

"Is that a swim suit I see?"

"Yeah." She picked at her nails.

"That's a great idea. Mind if I join you?"

"You have your swim suit on?"

"No, but it wouldn't be hard to put it on."

"I guess that's fine." She was being a little cold, but I could now see it was a front. She had felt bad about the fight too. It was obvious to me. I knew this was a stressful and confusing situation. Maybe swimming would be the relief we needed.

"How about I meet you out there then?"

"That would be fine." She picked up her towel and put her glasses down on her face, beginning to walk outside.

When I got out there, I had a hard time finding her. She was about shoulder deep in the waves, bobbing up and down as they crashed over and against her. They would push her towards shore, and she would swim back out, fighting against them. I joined her, showing her how to be caught in a wave, riding the top of it. She laughed a lot. She was becoming more and more relaxed and I was too.

The bridges of our noses began to burn red and she walked on the beach as I swam against the current for a while. The exercise helped take my mind off the morning. It made me feel strong, and although I was accomplishing nothing by beating against the waves, it made me feel like I had more energy than I had used. I felt powerful. I loved to test my strength, especially in nature.

Eventually there wasn't enough time left for us to enjoy the water. Though we were quiet, we walked back to the room together. I felt like lacing my fingers into hers, or like brushing her sandy hair behind her ears. I felt like singing a song and carrying her to our room, but I wasn't sure about that. I didn't know how she felt. I knew one thing was certain, if I found out she wasn't sold on me, and she didn't want me back, I was going to have to make her. A challenge that gave me more pleasure than discomfort, I was no stranger to wooing people over.

19

APRIL

I watched the sand and salt water wash down the drain. It trailed down my leg, in between my toes, and was swallowed by the hole in the tub. After rinsing down, it was time to get dressed for the party. I still wasn't sure what to wear, what to do with my hair or make up. Looking in the mirror, I saw my burn was already turning into a tan and my hair was half a shade lighter from being in the sun.

I had had a good time on the beach with Grant. It felt like we just went back into the natural swing of things, but I still had my reservations. I didn't know exactly what to say to him, and we hadn't talked about the fight since it had happened. My woman's intuition was in bad shape, and so I was stuck performing a routine for my apology in the mirror.

I didn't want him to be mad. I didn't know that he felt the same way towards me. I had never done anything like this, so I had no idea when to tell it was genuine or not. I was curious how tonight was going to go, after this morning went pretty well.

I started to think of a possible future with us. My parents already knew him, and he had the perfect story for his career. I wondered if he would quit his escort job for me. If he wasn't doing it for the money, what was he doing it for? I decided not to think about it. It was probably every man's dream to be paid heaping piles of cash for having sex with women.

I brushed the thoughts out of my head. I didn't want to get carried away with this. I wanted to be a few steps ahead. At the very least, I could maybe ask for a job as a secretary at his hedge fund. Then we could keep in contact and see how that goes.

I knew I was being silly. We had only known each other for a few days. He had sold me, though. I liked him a lot. How could someone resist? He was handsome, intelligent, dreamy, and pleasant. I could tell my parents were already impressed and Tom was envious. I liked that even more. The best revenge is being successful. This was me going to the top.

It was fun to have a little secret, doing a charade for these people. This was a stage, and this was my love scene. I felt weightless compared to the rest of the year. I was floating on a cloud, worry free. If all this went well, I would be better off than when I came here.

I wondered what his parents were like. He had told me something about them earlier, but they didn't talk much. He didn't seem close to them at all. I had the opposite experience. Is that what drove him to be an escort in the first place? Issues with his parents? I stopped drawing conclusions about him. I am sure there was a valid reason for his life. It could have even just been the thrill of adventure.

I went through my clothes, trying to figure out what would be the best thing to wear tonight. I buried the envelope that sat on top of my things deeper in the bag. I didn't mind keeping it at all. I decided to go with the nude and black maxi dress. I felt the most comfortable in it, and I wouldn't have to shave my legs, which I didn't have time for. I put my hair up in a bun and did a cat eye with red lips.

I rehearsed my apology once more before leaving the bathroom. I slipped on my heels and walked in the room. "You look lovely." I looked up from my feet. He was wearing a perfectly tailored suit with a dashing bow tie.

"You look... wow." He smiled when I said it. His perfectly white teeth glistened. He could be on a commercial or TV show. His hair was perfectly gelled back. My heart jumped. I could tell I was falling more and more for him. I could tell he felt the same by how he looked at me. We were going to give the bride and groom a run for their money with how great we would look together. "Listen, about last night," I started the apology "I am really sorry, I didn't – "

"Apology accepted." That was quick. I waited a bit for him to apologize too, but he stayed silent. I waited for a bit for him to say something. He straightened his tie and kept quiet. "What?"

"Aren't you going to say sorry too?"

"I don't see why I should."

"Really? After you threw that fit this morning?" I was surprised. I didn't want to fight again, but I thought I deserved some form of an apology.

"Nope. Besides, I've seen you throw a fit, too." He said, kidding. He lightly pushed me back twice until I fell onto the bed.

"Travis told me your real price. I can't believe... That's more money than I've made this year."

"Then you should appreciate what I've been doing for free." He smiled and kissed my cheek. I felt warm, and I had to fight to keep my hands from rushing up to touch the spot he kissed. He saw the shock in my face. He loved it. It fed him more and more. He kissed me again on the other cheek.

"We don't have a ton of time." I said. I wanted to make out, and I knew that was where he was leading, but if that led to sex we would be late for the party and I would have to redo my hair and makeup which would just take more time. It wasn't worth it.

"No, we don't." He said before kissing me on the mouth. He kissed me slowly, leaning over me. As he kissed me he pushed me back into the bed and crawled onto the bed himself, hovering over me. He put his hands on my waist and I wrapped my hands around his head, trying hard not to damage his perfectly done hair.

As he kissed me, I began to regret not shaving my legs. If he liked me as more than just a client, I'm sure that tonight would lead to more than just kissing. Weddings have a way of making everyone else sentimental about romance and love. I was no different, and would probably fall for the tricks of the ceremony.

If not, I would just be jaded by the fact it was my ex-fiancés wedding.

I push him away a little "We already spent so much time at the beach than we should have."

"That was fun." He started kissing my neck, very gently.

"You just keep trying to get me side tracked."

"Maybe just a little." He came over to me and put his hands on my shoulders. His thumbs rolled back and forth, rubbing my skin under the dress. His eyes looked hungry. I wanted him. He bit his teeth, fighting himself. It just made me want him more.

I wasn't over him yelling yet. I wasn't mad, and I understood why he was upset, but I thought that this was a two way road of problems. If he could drive me crazy for wanting him, I could do the same by resisting him. I lightly pushed him. His hands were freed from my shoulders.

He smiled, enjoying the fight. "I like you when you're feisty." He came back to me, kissing my cheek and trying to kiss my mouth. I stopped him, trying to speak with him.

"And you haven't said sorry yet."

"I think I'll make it up to you, somehow." He pulled my head towards his and kissed me again. This time I kissed back. I decided if I was going to be held hostage this weekend at a wedding, I was going to do it on my terms. We kissed and kissed and kissed.

He kissed my lips and then led over to my cheek, down my neck. It sent shivers down my spine, and I'm sure he loved that. He kissed me several times, going down to my collar bone. He kissed my collar bone. The fabric got between the two of us. I considered taking my dress off. As I lifted it up, he stopped me midway.

"We don't have any time. If you take it all off, I won't be able to stop." He rested the fabric around my waist and went down to my ankles. He kissed the inside of my ankles and worked up my calves to my knees. I was breathing quicker and quicker, trying not to get too loud. He kissed up more, kissing my knee cap as he worked up further, kissing a line up my thigh. I started to get nervous.

The anticipation was killing me. I wanted him. I was upset that we had started this, especially when we were so close to the wedding. I didn't appreciate him teasing me like this, but it felt so nice that I didn't stop him. I was going to force him to keep going later. He owed me that much.

He got to the outline of my panties, which were covered in black lace. With both hands, he pulled them down and slipped them off both of my legs. He kissed my hip. And then he moved his way down, putting a finger in me and licking the outside.

He kept going and going, hearing me sigh and moan, I could tell it only motivated him more. "We don't have time." I said. He didn't respond, just kept licking. His hand pulsed inside me, and I was being driven crazy. I wanted him, I wanted him, I wanted him.

I put my hands in his hair, I didn't care about messing up it up anymore. He didn't care about undressing me, after all. He worked harder and faster, and I could feel my pulse quicken. My back arched up and I fought back, trying not to give him the pleasure.

It got to a point where I couldn't fight it anymore. His fingers felt amazing. My toes curled. My mind went blank. I had the biggest orgasm that I have ever had. And from only him eating me out, I was in shock. Completely.

He was eating it up, loving that I went weak over him. He knew I wanted more. He knew that now that I had a taste, I was going to get hungrier. He began to slow down, weaning me off. I took this time to gather myself, and try to remember what planet I was on.

"That was pretty good." I heaved, breathing every word.

"I wish we had more time." He said. He kissed his way back down my leg, slower than he had before.

"That was… Really good." I could feel him smile when he kissed. He slipped the panties back on my legs. "That was a first."

"First time someone has gone down on you?"

"No." I sassed back. I knew he thought I was innocent, but just because I wasn't as experienced as him didn't mean that I hadn't experienced some things. "First time that it has made me, uh…"

"Orgasm?"

"Yeah." I pulled the panties the rest of the way up and hopped off the bed. I fixed my hair and makeup in the mirror. It hadn't gotten too ruffled, so I wouldn't kill him. I saw him perched on the bed, fixing his own hair and smiling from ear to ear.

PART 4

20

GRANT

Following her down to the lobby was driving me crazy. I was pretty aroused from earlier, and looking at the back of her wasn't helping. She peeked over at me, her face was gorgeous. The makeup highlighted her features, and having her hair pulled back drew attention to it. She was gorgeous. I hadn't seen someone as naturally beautiful as her.

Her dress perfectly complimented my suit. We looked fantastic together. I'm sure we would turn all the heads. We might even take all the attention from the bride and groom. Hand in hand, we glided into the dimly lit room. Tables were softly lit by the centerpieces, and the shadows of the candles danced on the floor. The room was decorated with drapes that made it look like clouds were floating on the sides of the room. The windows showed the early evening sun warming up the ocean, getting ready to take a dip into the night. I hadn't been to a place this beautiful in a while. Weddings were always so elegant, but this one had a lot of them beat. Even the times before when I had been to this hotel, it had never seemed this dapper.

Tonight was already a great night, and this scenery was making it perfect. We were going to dance. We had to. The band set up. We were there early. We should have stayed in our room for a little while longer. I kept thinking back to before and it drove me crazy. I wanted to go back upstairs and fling her on the bed. I wanted to show her all my learned skills. I wanted her to feel special.

She rubbed my thumb with hers, and it felt so sweet and gentle. April was perfect. We kept hands linked as we walked through the room, greeting everyone. I just kept thinking of before, how her legs relaxed and toes curled. I had felt her hands grabbing at the sheets and I couldn't get the scene out of my head. It gave me butterflies. I loved pleasing women, that was why I was in this line of business. Pleasing April magnified that. I was proud. I felt like a million dollars. Even if she didn't want to see me after this weekend, at least I would be one of her firsts, and therefore made permanent in her memories.

We saw the heads turn as we passed through the tables to ours. She smiled. It radiated. This weekend would do wonders for her confidence. "You look lovely." I whispered in her ear.

She smiled. "You keep saying that."

"It's true."

We got to our table and sat by her parents. I wanted to make a good impression, but I was still sidetracked by thoughts I had about us earlier. I held her hand as I spoke with her mom. Her fingers belonged in my hair, ruffling it up. I spoke about my hedge fund to her parents. It was all fairly boring business stuff, but I knew they would be impressed by it. I kept talking about the success of the business without being too proud. I had performed this dialogue enough times that I had it memorized. It rolled off my tongue as I thought about April in bed. I wanted her again. I wanted her now. I could imagine her body under the outline of her clothes. The image was burned into my mind. It spun in loops, driving me crazy.

When I had exhausted the business talk I thought I would have a moment to think. Her mom kept speaking. I could tell she was charmed by me, she kept asking me more and more about my life, trying to dissect my brain and pull all the information out.

"You are doing very well for yourself." Her dad said, raising a glass to me.

"Thank you, sir."

"Now, I bet you were raised by a great family, tell me about your parents." Her mom said, taking a drink of her champagne.

"Well, they actually are in a different line of business." I looked to April, wondering if I should be telling this much detail about my life. It made it more realistic, but I wasn't ready to have my book opened. I got over that quick. I was here on work. I had to do my job. "They have significant interest in a casino in Vegas. That's where we are from."

"And what about your mother?"

I didn't want to say they were divorced. That would ruin the magic of my allure. I decided it was for the best to talk about my parents in the most positive light, even if it was lying. "My mom helps him."

In reality she wanted nothing to do with my dad. After he was having another kid, she would refuse to be in the same room with him. She thought it was gross. She shamed him every time they had to meet. I couldn't say any of that. I had to paint a dazzling picket fence life.

"Which casino is it?" Her dad asked.

"Are you a card player?" I asked, trying to detour their questions. I didn't want to give too much info away.

"Not at all. I dabble with friends, but I wouldn't dare try professionally."

"Enough." Her mom said. She lightly slapped his thigh. "Which casino was it, Grant?"

"It's called Oasis. It has an Egyptian theme. It's sort of corny. My dad was inspired by Indiana Jones. It was fun to run around there when I was a kid."

"I'm sure." She finished her drink. "I have actually heard of this casino. Isn't it a hotel as well?"

"Yes actually."

"Did you have any siblings to run around with you?"

This whole while April was paying attention to me. I could tell she liked having them off her back. I was fine with the questions, but I could see how she was exhausted by them. "I have a few older brothers."

"Are they in the casino business too?"

"Not quite. Actually my oldest brother just opened up a new hotel."

"That's exciting. Do you get to go for free?"

"I don't know. I'll have to ask." I assumed that I would. I don't think my brother would care too much for me visiting, though. Not when he was up to his ears with paperwork for the new building.

"Maybe you can take April on a little trip." April flushed. Her mom kept talking. "Where is it at?"

"It's in Seattle."

"Wouldn't you like that, honey? That would be fun." Her mom finally addressed April. She was spacing off a bit, but turned her head quickly towards her mother.

"Yeah, that would be nice. I don't want to barge, though." She said. I could tell she was treating it as a real proposition. I wondered if I could actually convince her to go somewhere with me.

"It wouldn't be barging at all. I'd love to have your company." We made eye contact, locking our eyes for a while. I meant it. I genuinely did. I wanted to tour the world, holding her on a pedestal. She was gorgeous and smart. I couldn't stop thinking about her when she left the room. When she was getting ready for tonight, I sat outside the bathroom, waiting to surprise her.

Her mom chimed back in, asking me more and more questions about my life. She was like a detective, trying to pin down every second of my life. April went back to spacing off as I answered the questions. I wondered what she was thinking about. Was she remembering earlier, holding onto the moment as much as I was?

Not much more time had passed before April's mom began to talk to her dad. They talked about Vegas and the last time they went there. I started to tune them out, paying more attention to April. I could tell something was distracting her, and she looked a little bothered. I didn't know what by. I squeezed her hand in mine, hoping it would let her know that it was going to be okay.

The room was beginning to fill with more people. It was getting harder and harder to hear April's parents. I didn't mind it. I liked having some time to think. I wondered if April wanted to go on the trip. Her hesitation could have been genuine too. It was hard to tell what she really wanted from me. I knew we had something, but I didn't know how long she would let the fling last.

She seemed totally uninterested in Tom now. She didn't look at him once this whole time. I kept my eye on them, though. I waited for him to swoop in like a hawk, trying to take her as his prey. He seemed so conflicted about his relationship. I wasn't about to let him make mine more complicated than it already was.

I wanted April to be happy, but I knew he was no good for her. I think she knew that, too. She had been cold to him this morning, and you could tell there was still some resentment to him. It wasn't her fault. He shouldn't have been a dick to her. If I weren't here to wow everyone, I probably would have given him a piece of my mind. The closest I could come now is bragging about April and I's pretend happy life. It was enough for me.

It started to give me actual thoughts about our future, too. I wanted to keep her around. I wanted to help her through her tough time. I wanted to show her that she was more important than she felt, that she could achieve much more. April needed to feel valuable, and even though she was becoming more confident, you could tell she was still embarrassed and disappointed in herself. I didn't know if she got that from her parent's high expectations, or from Tom's good fortune but it didn't matter to me. And it shouldn't matter to her. This was her life, and they didn't have to be involved if they were just bringing her down.

Her mom began to talk to me again about Vegas. She talked about how she missed the city. She asked me for all kinds of stories, wanting to know the craziest things that had happened. I kept my eye on April as I spoke, and April seemed invested. She laughed when the stories were funny and looked at me to show interest.

The music started up. I tried talking over it, but it proved to be difficult. As more and more people filtered in the room, the louder the music became and the more isolated I felt. Even just sitting here was making me feel antsy. Normally I was good with weddings and wedding parties, but I was becoming restless. I wanted to talk to April more. I wanted to figure out what was wrong, and I wanted to take her upstairs and escape all these people.

But that wasn't going to happen. The party hadn't even started yet. I sat back and talked more and more about Vegas. I hoped that it made April interested. I would love to have her over. I could take her all over the town. She was the only female who I was close to that didn't have grey roots. I was smitten. She was very different. She had the potential to grow. She just needed someone to show her that. I would happily be that person.

21

APRIL

I was pretty nervous. Lucky for me, Grant was doing all the talking. If I spoke, I knew that I would have a panic attack. I didn't think I could handle this. It was a lot to go through, and adrenaline coursed through my veins. I could use a drink. Maybe five. Grant kept talking to my mom, keeping her tamed and away from asking me about life and work and death. The way Grant spoke was reassuring. I didn't want him to be gone after this weekend. I knew we had so much more than we were accepting.

The chatter rose and I kept spacing out. I was still flustered from before. I had never had a guy that was so good at making me climax. I tried not to think about it too much. When I did, it just reminded me of his line of work. I didn't want to think about how many women he had been with. I didn't want to think about why he did what he did. I just wanted to think about him as a person, the hedge fund owner that was wowing my parents.

Tom began approaching our table. My pulse rose, my hands became clammy. I removed them from Grant's intertwined fingers for the first time since we left the room. "Oh no." I whispered. Grant looked at him approaching and let out a deep breath. He went back to speaking to my parents, making my mom laugh, and telling her about all the great adventures he had had in Vegas.

I wanted to put on an invisibility shield. I wanted Tom to just leave me alone. He didn't seem to care or think so. He jogged over to our table and greeted everyone. "April, could I pull you aside for a second?"

"Fine." I got up and pushed my chair back in. I leaned over to Grant. "I'll only be a moment. Save me if I am gone for too long."

"You'll be fine. Take your time." I wanted Grant to come with. He could be a body guard for my heart. Tom was just going to toy with me and disappoint me. He seemed to love doing that. I began picking at my fingers, walking behind Tom to a secluded part of the room where it was a bit quieter.

"What?"

"I just wanted to talk to you. I didn't get to say that much this morning." He flushed. I knew he knew that I didn't want to be there, trapped with him in the corner of the room. I had no choice. It was his party. "So, you two seem pretty happy."

"We are. You seem happy as well."

"Do I?" This sounded like an actual question, not like the snide remarks that I expected from him.

"Yes. Congratulations. She is gorgeous."

"Thank you." There was a lull in the speaking. I kept my arms crossed. It grew awkward, but I had nothing to respond with. I wasn't the one that asked for the conversation. I didn't want to be here to begin with. This wasn't on me. "To be honest, I'm not really sure I want to go through with this."

I was surprised to hear it. It hurt me. I couldn't believe him. Did marriage mean nothing? First me, and now that hottie? I didn't know her, but she seemed like a very nice girl. "Oh? Calling off weddings is too much fun for you?"

"What was that?" He genuinely didn't hear me.

"I said why do you want to call it off?"

He paused and looked at his bride to be for a bit. "I don't know if I do want to call it off. I just don't know if I am ready yet." This was typical Tom. He could never commit to anything. I saw how confused he was. I felt bad, but I didn't know how to help him. This was some much deeper issue that I didn't have enough experience to help with.

"Then you shouldn't have proposed."

"Yeah. Well. It was complicated."

I saw the crack in his perfect life. The foundation to his hard exterior was faltering and I was here to see it crumble. His eyes grew wet. He stopped talking. "What's going on?" I became more concerned the more his brows furrowed. He was really having a difficult time.

After a second he took a deep breath. "I don't know. I was pressured into this sort of. Or, at least I feel pressured. I don't know."

"Oh. That's not good. You two seem so happy, though. What's the problem?" he seemed so in love and ready to marry her when he spammed my timeline with photos and posts about her all the time. It was as if nothing else went on in his life. Just the thrill and excitement of expensive vacations with one of the prettiest girls in California.

"When I asked her to marry me, I did it out of necessity." He was still hesitant to tell me. What did that mean? Did he feel the same way when he proposed to me? Like I needed it for reassurance? I had actually loved him. When I said yes it was because I had thought about spending the rest of my life with him years before he showed me a ring. I felt sick to my stomach. I didn't want to have to coach him through his wedding after he shattered me before mine.

"What do you mean?"

"She said that she was pregnant." He dropped the bomb. I didn't want to hear that. He had always been so careful. I couldn't imagine him not using protection. Even when I was on the pill he would use it, just in case. He was never ready to be responsible for another person. That was an even bigger commitment than marriage. "I couldn't have that happen. I loved her enough that I thought it could work, but now she isn't pregnant anymore. I don't know if she ever was. But I can't go back on it, because then our parents will ask. My mom and dad were already furious at me when we...."

"Yeah." He didn't have to say anything. I knew. I had loved his parents like they were my own. They treated me like family. I was certain that I was going to become family. They must have felt the same way. I wondered if they liked her as much as they liked me. I wondered if they were just being nice to me. They were such sweet people, Tom could have brought in a homeless person and they would be head over heels for them.

"But you seem to be having such a great time with Grant that I wanted your advice. What keeps you two going? I know it's probably early in your relationship, but I have to wonder. Are you two doing well?" The way he said it made me feel like he had other motives. He looked at me with hope. It made me even sicker.

I thought about his question. I wanted to help Tom, but at the same time I didn't want him to feel like he could stomp me until I was a pulp of a person. He had already caused enough emotional damage. I didn't need to become his relationship therapist for this one. And I didn't want to become his rebound. I didn't want him anymore.

"Love." I said. I stopped picking my fingers.

"Genuine, unfaltering love. He and I may have difficult times, sure. But even when we fight, we keep what's important in our thoughts. We just want to be happy with each other, no matter what it takes. I have never felt such a powerful amount of emotion for one person. I am in love like never before." I could see the daggers I threw at him cut him.

"When we make decisions, we know that it is because we want to, and not because we feel like we have to. We love each other."

I looked over to Grant. He was still chatting with my mom, making her and my father laugh. I wasn't in love, not yet. But I could see myself falling for him. I looked back at Tom, the person I used to love. I knew all his strengths and weaknesses. I had been with him through thick and thin. When I looked at him now I didn't feel anything. When I looked at Grant, I could feel sparks.

"I don't know if she and I have that."

"You better find out soon. It's about to become legally recognized." I did have some pity on him. It would be hard to be stuck in a relationship without love. It would be hard to be stuck in a relationship period. Without love, he would become bitter and either have to get a divorce or stay unhappily married if he waited too long.

"You guys do so many fun things, though. I wouldn't have guessed you weren't happy. Your Instagram streams are flooded with smiles and what seems like exotic vacations. How do you know it isn't just cold feet?"

"I don't know that. But there are a lot of issues, too. Those have been there for a while."

"Well, I'm not a therapist. But if you want help, there are people out there that can help you." The party began, and people at the front started giving speeches for the two of them. Tom listened intently. I looked for his fiancée. She was sitting at the front, looking for Tom. "You should go stand by her at least." I said.

"I'm fine back here." He still listened. A lot of her friends spoke, saying that they couldn't have asked for a better guy for the bride. He would clap and laugh when appropriate, but I could see the pain in his eyes. This was one battle that I didn't have to help him through.

Out of the corner of my eye I saw Grant get up. He came over to us and said hi to Tom. Tom said hi back and went back to listening to the speeches, but he watched us out of his peripherals. Grant smiled at me.

"Hey."

"Hi."

He put his arm around my shoulder and pulled me in close to him. I looked into his eyes. I saw a man. More man than Tom. I saw someone who wanted to make others happy. I saw someone who did things for other people not because he had to, but because he wanted to. I saw someone that I wanted to keep seeing over and over again.

He was being very understanding about Tom. I appreciated that so much. He no longer actually needed to be here with me, but he chose to. It was nice to have someone with me to fight this battle. I was lucky that it was Grant. He noticed me staring and smiled back.

"Hey." He said, again.

"Hi." I repeated. I was falling for him. How could I not fall for him? He was kind, dashing, and he had already won over my parents. This was the easiest relationship I had ever been in. I wanted it to last. I wanted to rub my happiness in Tom's face.

Grant excused us and we went back to the table. He ordered a couple drinks, sensing that me talking to Tom wasn't what I had wanted to do. He asked me multiple times to make sure I was okay. I was. I felt better for sticking it to Tom. I felt better that his life wasn't as perfect as it seemed. It made me feel less awful about mine. It gave me hope. Maybe everyone was going through pretty shitty times. It didn't just have to be me.

All of the bride's family and friends were beautiful too. They were the majority of the people who spoke that night. I recognized a few of Tom's friends, but most of these people were strangers to me. It seemed like he had started a new life with her, and had a clean slate after me.

I grabbed Grant's hand and then excused us again from the table. The party wasn't over, but I was done with it. I pulled him back to the room.

22

GRANT

After talking to Tom, April was more and more interested in me. I was so relieved. I was worried that he would try to win her back. I'm glad he didn't. When we got back to the room she immediately kicked off her shoes and led me to the bed. My pulse was racing again. I was so thrown back by her abrasiveness that it gave me butterflies. I felt cheery and I also kicked off my shoes.

She pulled me in by my neck, kissing me. She tasted like cherries. She was lovely. I began to pull at my belt, but she took my hands and gently rested them on her waist. She was so soft. I wanted to shock her. I was going to. I was going to drive her wild.

I grabbed at her waist and leaned over her again. I kissed and kissed, my heart racing more and more. As it went on, I began to kiss her faster and harder. She gasped under the kisses. I moved my hands to her back and let my tongue into her mouth, twirling it over and over around hers. She sighed.

I wanted her so bad. I wanted her now. I was going to have to make it last, though. I was going to milk every minute of this, enjoying all of her body. She was so curvy. She was hot. I pulled at my belt again, this time getting it out of my pants.

April pulled back, letting down her hair and shaking it back and forth. The bun had curled the ends of it into gentle waves. She was stunning. She looked at me through heavy lidded eyes. "You're so sexy." I whispered. She smiled and pulled me back in. I kissed her neck. She let her head fall to the side and took every bit of it with pleasure. She smelled like lilacs. Her hair was soft. I pushed my hands into it, feeling all of it. She sighed again.

I couldn't handle it when she made noise. It made me harder and harder. I hadn't been this aroused before. I wanted to have her. I wanted her bad. I stopped kissing her and went back down to her feet, lifting her dress. This time I lifted it over her head. He bra didn't match her panties. It was adorable. I kissed her neck and started to work my way down. I kissed her breast. Unhooking her bra, I pulled it off with my teeth. I was going to use all the tricks I could to impress her.

"Very talented," she giggled. She sighed as I resumed kissing. I sucked on her softly. Her legs wriggled beneath me and I felt her hands grip at my hair. I was becoming harder and harder as she did, letting out soft moans as I kept kissing.

She pulled me up to her face, using her hands to unbutton my shirt. I pulled off my tie, tossing it to the floor. Her hair was already a little bit crazy, and it just turned me on more.

I let the shirt slide off my arms and pulled off my under shirt quickly. Leaning to the side, I slid my hands down her waist and into her underwear. They were wet. I played with her, going in circles. My fingers danced, and she breathed heavier, hanging on my lips with hers. Her hands worked quickly, unbuttoning my pants and unzipping them. She felt me from outside of my underwear, stroking me slowly.

I bit her lip. It made her gasp. I couldn't help myself at all. I moved to her ears and sucked softly on the lobe. She sighed again, and rubbed faster and faster.

I pushed her underwear down, in hopes she would do the same with mine. She didn't. She stroke harder and harder. I put my fingers in her, pulsing back and forth. She rocked with me, grabbing my arm with one of her hands. She squeezed and moaned louder.

"Take my pants off." I whispered to her. She opened her eyes and slowly lowered my pants to my bent knees. I kicked them back. "Now the boxers." I watched her as she lifted the band and pushed them down too. My dick was hard. I rolled a condom from my pocket down on it.

She spread her legs, bending them at the knees. I pushed into her gently, thrusting slowly. She put her hands on my neck and pulled me into her, kissing me. She was tight. I took my hand and moved it down to her clit, playing with it as I humped her. She moaned louder and louder.

I couldn't help myself. I went faster and faster. I loved the way she sounded. It was so hot. I caught myself sighing, too. She pulled me in hard, and I started kissing her harder. She rolled over and sat on top of me.

She pushed with so much force. I didn't expect that. When she bounced, her boobs bounced with her. I put my hands on them, gently playing with her nipples. She kept sighing and kept bouncing, growing louder and louder.

She kept beating on me, harder and harder until she started moaning very loudly. The headboard beat against the wall. I could feel myself bubbling up. I put my hands on her thighs and pushed from the bottom.

I bit my lip. My pulse was high. I felt her hot and wet on me. She rocked back and forth, spinning around and around on top of me.

I pushed her back over and went back on top. Holding her legs up, I humped faster than I had before. I went deep, all the way in. Until I came. It sent chills down my spine. She grabbed at my back, leaving marks where her fingers had been. I humped a few more times until I pulled out.

I had never experienced sex that was that great, or at least, not for a very very very long time. She panted on the bed, exhausted and sweating. She was so adorable.

"That was something." She breathed, pushing her hair behind her ears.

I couldn't speak. I was overwhelmed. I just kissed her on the mouth. It sent more chills down my back. I hadn't felt this way in a long time. I didn't know what love felt like, but this was the closest I had gotten.

She pulled back and smiled at me. After kissing my sweaty forehead she went to the bathroom and put her pajamas on. Even though the TV played shows, I was distracted. I thought of her. I wondered what we would do after this weekend. I wanted to see her frequently. I wanted to see her forever.

She fell asleep quickly so I turned the TV off. Tucking her in, I kissed her forehead. Even though I had been upset earlier, I was happy to have met her. I felt like I should have been the one paying this time. It was a magical weekend.

I had a hard time going to sleep. Thoughts of earlier kept racing though my head and gave me more butterflies than before. Remembering the moments would make me hard enough alone. I wanted her again, but couldn't stand to wake her up. I went to bed after a while. She looked so peaceful next to me.

23

APRIL

I didn't realize my phone was ringing at first. I thought it was a melody that was part of my dream. My sleep-crusted eyes shot open as soon as I figured out that I wasn't prancing in a meadow. I must have forgotten to turn off an alarm, or maybe I accidentally set one. Grant stirred. For a second I thought I had woke him up. He turned over and continued to breathe his long and heavy sleep breaths. My screen was like sunlight through a magnifying glass to my eyes. Squinting through my eyelids, I saw I had one missed call. It was from Tom.

I let out a heavy, heaping sigh. There must have been some rule of etiquette he was breaking about the amount of times he had talked to his ex-fiancée at his current engagement party.

I snuck out of the room, slowly and as quietly as I could. I didn't want to wake Grant. I didn't want him to think that I was weak for encouraging Tom. I wasn't encouraging him. I didn't want him to call me. It was exhausting to be here and not away from the terror of his presence. I thought I had missed him. Now I miss the days where I could go hours without thinking about him once. Or at least, without seeing him once.

Almost as soon as I let the door lightly click shut my phone began to ring again. It was Tom again, right on queue. I slid my finger over the screen and answered.

"Hello?"

"April?"

"It's six in the morning."

"Hi. I know. Sorry. Good morning."

"Hi?" I knew there had to be more to this than a wakeup call. There always was something that made what could have been simple infinitely more complex. "It's six in the morning?" I said it like a question. I was unable to phrase all of my real questions. If I hadn't woken up only moments ago, maybe I would have been smart enough to just turn my phone on silent.

"I know. I said sorry." There was his snark.

"Couldn't you have texted? Or waited to call when humans are awake?"

"I need to see you. Now." He said it like a command. "This can't wait any longer."

"Is someone in trouble or something?"

"...No."

"Is there an emergency?"

"Yes." I could tell he was lying.

"Is there an emergency that requires my immediate attention?"

"I need to see you now." He said again. "Come down to the lobby."

My only course of action was to follow. I sighed heavily. It seemed to be the only thing I was in control of anymore. I could only express myself through insignificant signs of annoyance. "Fine." I pushed the door open slightly, hoping even more now not to wake Grant. I kicked flip flops on and then exited the room as quietly as I could.

The elevator ride was long. My brain was now processing at a speed where I could frantically worry about everything. My stomach turned in knots. I made a mental list of all the things in the world I didn't want to do right now.

10. Get lost in the sewers of LA

9. Pluck out each of my leg hairs individually

8. Be water boarded

7. Get burned at the stake for being a witch

6. Fight my way out of a rainforest

5. Get stranded on a desert island, inhabited by cannibals

4. Retake my final exams

3. Live in a world of flesh eating zombies

2. Go to Tom's Engagement party

1. Talk to Tom

I looked at the red button on the elevator. I could force it down and get locked in here. I wouldn't have to think of any of this for at least one hour. I could turn the inside of the elevator into a tiny house and show it off to HGTV. I could be the woman who famously made an elevator into an adorable abode.

The numbers on the elevator counted down. I did nothing but stare at them as they initiated my inevitable doom. The lobby floor dinged. The doors parted, opening on an almost empty lobby, the only inhabitants being hotel staff doing their morning chores and Tom, sitting at a table where you had a direct view of the elevators. I had no choice but to sit by him now. He saw me.

With each step I considered a new escape plan. "I have a call from the president. I need to take it." No, it needed to be more realistic.

"My dad is having a heart attack and my mom is having a stroke." Too realistic and too morbid.

"I have explosive diarrhea." That one was good. That was realistic. People experienced that. I can pretend that.

Several tiny steps and deep breaths later and I was at his table, staring in the eyes of the beast. He smiled up at me, his fangs gleaming, ready to snap the neck of his prey, me. I stood, frozen.

"Hi April." I said nothing I stood, staring at him. If I made myself look larger than him, maybe that would scare him away. I could puff up my chest and growl.

"I forgot how nice you look without makeup."

What a smoozer. I hated him. I hated his dumb face that looked so happy on Instagram. In front of me, though, he didn't look so thrilled. I could see worry lines on his forehead and his brows seemed heavier than usual. I stood my ground, still frozen before him.

"Do you want to sit down? This could take a bit."

I sat, putting my palms on my lap. As soon as they were out of his line of sight I immediately began picking at my nails. I would need to wear them down to the nubs to get through this conversation.

"What's the emergency?" I said, with no feeling in my voice. I was able to keep it from quivering. I had an idea of what he wanted. I knew what he was going to say. He was going to try and hurt me. He was going to make me feel lower than I had since he left. He was going to rub it in my face that I wasn't happy, that I wasn't living out some dream life like he was. I looked at his palms on the table. He had also been picking at his nails and moved on to chewing on them. I didn't know what to say to him so I just repeated myself. "What's the emergency? What couldn't wait till daylight?"

"I need you, April." He coughed out through teeth clenched around his nails.

My heart stopped then resumed beating, pumping faster than it had ever pumped before. I couldn't believe my ears. I knew that he hadn't hated me by the way he acted at the past two parties, but hearing that was too much to handle. I had to be hallucinating. Was I still dreaming?

I didn't know what to say. I said nothing. I looked at him, biting the ends of his fingers. "What?"

"I miss you."

"Uh…"

"Hear me out. I know I don't deserve you back. I don't even deserve to be friends with you. I ruined what we had and I'm sorry. It's just the accident was hard on me too…" He looked me in the eyes for a brief moment. His gaze switched back to the empty table in front of us.

"I just didn't know that you were what was missing. I felt like I had this… this void in my life. I was looking all over the place to fill it. I thought maybe my job would help, and it did for a while but all that joy has left me. To be honest, I don't know how long I'm going to have that job anyway. So then when the job didn't work, I thought that maybe I was just lonely. And I think I was. And now, looking at you and what you have I… Well, seeing you with Grant made me realize how much I miss you. I knew I had lost a good thing, I just didn't know that It was meant to be." He reached his hands under the table and clasped mine. His palms were sweaty and hot. I couldn't stand the way they felt on me.

"You complete me, April."

We sat there for a long time in silence. I had no idea what to do. Had I have come to this alone, I would have taken him back immediately. Of course, he wouldn't have wanted me because I wasn't alone. Now when I looked across the table I didn't see some perfect man who left me for a better person. I saw a child who was unable to make up his mind. He just wanted the toys other kids were playing with, no matter what toy he had. It was never enough. Travis was right.

"No." I said quietly. I didn't know what else to say. I didn't have anything else to say. I saw his eyes. They welled up with water.

"What?"

I didn't respond. He let the tears drop out, burying his head into his palms. He was crying. Sobbing. This is exactly what a child would have done if you had taken their once special toy away, moments after they have left it in the dirt. We sat there, speechless at the table. The only sound filling the lobby was Tom's gasping cries.

"I should have known." He stuttered out. "I should have known better than to make a fool of myself. I just saw his face and I saw your face. And I knew. I knew that I made you that happy before. And you. You made me that happy. We were so good. Why did I give you up? I should have known. I should have held onto you. And now you're doing better. You have the perfect job and the perfect boyfriend. You're going to be successful and famous and some day you won't even remember my name. You and Grant." He choked as he spoke. "You two are going to live in some great big mansion and go on trips and get married and live the happily ever after ending that is only in fairytales."

"No." I said again. This time, it was with more remorse in my voice. He stopped babbling.

His lips quivered as he looked at me. "What?"

"We won't have that life." I said. It was true. We wouldn't have that life. No one would. No one could. I had thought that if anyone were capable of it, it would have been him. I realized that fairytales weren't based on life. They were just based on glimpses of reality. No one had a happy perfect life. Everyone just lived their best version of one. The world would never allow for perfect people or perfect things. If it had, then life would be boring and eventless, ever person already paired off from beginning to end. There would be no art and no reason to have art. We would be like animals. "Grant and I aren't all you make us up to be."

His face turned again. It was red and blotchy with shiny stains were the tears had ran down. "Yes you are. I know you guys aren't perfect, but he has you. You're perfect. You just aren't perfect together."

My mind was spinning. I had to stop him from saying anymore while I could. "Me and Grant have nothing to do with you and your future."

"No. But you have everything to do with my future. I'll be a mess without you."

"No, you don't understand. Grant and I… we aren't what it looks like."

He sniffed. "What do you mean?"

"Grant didn't want to come to this."

He chuckled a little. I could feel the lump in my neck. It was going to be harder than I thought to comfort Tom. "I can't blame him for not wanting to come. I wouldn't want to go to your wedding, and I know that …"

"No. You don't understand." I said again. I looked into his eyes, blood shot and red. I didn't want to say it. I tried to signal to him, to beg with my face for him not to make me say it. He looked more confused than ever. "Grant isn't all that he seems."

"I don't understand." He said. His face was puffy and swollen from crying, but the tears had stopped.

"No, you don't. Grant… He is an escort. He isn't… He…" I couldn't form words. I started to babble as badly as he was. I wished that if I could take it back. I wondered if maybe I said enough words he would have just forgotten everything I had said. Was it too late to use the diarrhoea line? Would that distract him?

"A what?"

I said nothing. I picked at my fingers more. I noticed blood was starting to pool out from beneath one of my nails. I shouldn't have said anything. This awful day was already getting worse and it wasn't even time for breakfast. The silence made me feel guilt. I wished the music were still playing. I wish that there was some bustle or bang from the staff. I would have taken the sound of a rocket taking off over this. Anything to fill the void.

The elevator dinged and we both looked to the doors. As they parted, the last person I wanted to see was standing in there, looking confused and hurt. Grant looked out at us, sitting at a table in the lobby, me in a robe and Tom in his pajamas. I could tell that there was going to be big problems. Grant's charm wasn't turned on, instead we saw the raw and vulnerable Grant that rarely showed himself. Especially on business.

He walked slowly and calmly to our table. Tom's red eyes were large, watching each movement that was made. I was frozen again. I didn't know what to say. I didn't know how to speak. I had lost the ability to communicate completely. Tom was the first one to break the silence.

"Are you kidding me? You're dating a whore?" Tom was frantic, shouting at the both of us. Grant's stone face dropped into a frown. He gave me a disappointed look and walked to our table quicker. He starred at Tom. "You're dating a fucking hooker? That's what your life has stooped to? I can't believe this. You have to be kidding me." He stood up and walked the rest of the way to Grant, his hands balled in fists. Once he was feet away I realized what he was charging at Grant to do.

I yelled at him to stop, but it was too late. He swung his fist, missing Grant's face. Grant dodged back and grabbed his hand. He punched him in the face with his other hand and Tom fell back to the ground.

I ran over to him immediately. His eyes were shut and he was limp on the floor. "Tom? Tom, can you hear me?" I held his head in my lap and looked up at Grant.

Grant said nothing. He only looked down at us. His face was stone again. I couldn't tell what he was feeling. I had no idea what I was supposed to say to him. I was upset. I was furious with Tom but I was still upset with Grant. I hated violence. Tom was a kid, he didn't know how to control himself. I didn't know what happened with Grant. His face was impossible to read.

I kept tapping Tom, trying to get his attention. Grant turned on his heels and left, going back into the elevator. I didn't know why he came down in the first place. He must have been looking for me. I should have just stayed in the room. I didn't know I was going to ruin our time. I needed to tell Grant that it wasn't what it looked like. Or maybe it was.

The point was I didn't want Tom back. I didn't know that was why Tom needed me either. There was so much I had to say to Grant still. I kept tapping Tom, trying to get his attention. He was still breathing and his finger twitched. He slowly came to and I helped him back up on his feet.

I pushed the number to our floor several times. I paced back and forth in the elevator with Tom. He held a Kleenex to his nose and watched me as I planned my speech for Grant in my head. The doors were taking too long to close. The elevator was taking too long to move. I tapped the button several more times. I knew it wouldn't change anything, but I needed something to do.

My palms were sweaty. My mind was racing. I could tell Tom was annoyed by me. I could see that he was mad that I was worried about Grant. I didn't care. Maybe that would help get him to back off. When we got to the floor the doors spread open and I jogged to my room. I pushed the key in several times before it worked.

I walked in. I didn't see his suitcase. I checked the door of the dresser. All his things were gone.

24

GRANT

I waited in the airport for hours for the next available flight. It gave me time to cool down. I had never lost my temper like that before. I had never punched another guy. I was glad that if I was ever going to only punch one person, it was Tom.

My knuckles were bruised and I took it as a badge of honor. I put ice on them, hoping it would keep the swelling down. It was expensive to fly last minute from Santa Barbra to Las Vegas. I didn't care. I had more than enough money. I didn't want to spend another moment here, even if that meant taking coach.

I was mad at Tom. He deserved what he got. I had been waiting to punch him since I had heard about him. I never would have thought I would have gotten a golden opportunity like that.

Whatever April saw in him, I was blind to. She could run off to him. I didn't care. I was so disappointed. She wasn't the smart woman I thought she had been. If she fell for a doof like that, there must have been something I was missing.

I didn't know why she went back to him. We were having a great time. We were having a perfect time. I thought that maybe we were starting to have a spark. I could have seen myself seeing her several times within the next month. I could have seen myself asking her out formally.

I fell for her spell. I must have been distracted by her beauty. I had thought she had been perfect. I was told that she was great. I didn't understand why she wasn't getting any jobs. I also didn't understand why someone would leave her. There had to be something.

She got what she wanted after all. She got Tom back. She could go back to living her happy perfect life from before her accident. She could get re-engaged and marry someone on the verge of bankruptcy. They could be homeless together and be clueless and hopeless people.

This was the first weekend I lost money being an escort. It was also going to be the last time. I wasn't going to whore my services out for friends anymore. I would never do a sexual favor for free again. I had standards.

The plane was called and I watched the movie they played on the way back. It was one of those romantic comedies that was really popular in the early 2000s. I hadn't seen it before, but I remembered the commercials and I remembered knowing women that liked it.

I needed a drink. I hated romantic comedies. No matter how honest they tried to be, they were still just a story. I watched the same imperfect beginning end with the same perfect ending in other movies time and time again. It was boring, predictable, and old. It never happened that way in real life. And when it did, there was still a ton of shit that had to be worked through.

And they never put in the troubles. They never had the relationship after a few years. They didn't put in the couples therapy or the divorce that happened if the therapy didn't help. They didn't put in affairs or anything but good feeling and light humor. I wanted to live in a Walt Disney world like that. I wanted to live in a world where my greatest pleasure wasn't being an escort and I didn't feel so god damn lonely.

Meg Ryan was on the screen, denying her inevitable future. That's what the characters always did. They fought the happiness until they no longer could. They wanted to be upset. It made it a tunnel vision, like a relationship would fix all the problems you didn't know you were having. It didn't work that way in real life.

In real life your romantic interest left you for their douche of an ex-fiancé because their self-confidence is low. In real life there wasn't a big character change or happy ending, just a ton of small changes and tiny victories.

I counted this weekend as a loss except for the punch. It was well worth it. Even if it had broken my hand, which I am glad it didn't, I would have done it again.

I wasn't sure what to do with my life after this trip. I wasn't sure I even wanted to be an escort anymore. Maybe I should move back to California, or somewhere else on the coast. I would love to swim. I had more than enough money and time. Even if I just did it for a year, it would be worth it to get away and reevaluate everything for a while.

I looked online at condos. I tried to find one with a small lease. If all else failed, I could just stay in a hotel. I would have originally stayed with Alex, but now it would be too big of a risk to run into April.

I could run away from my parents and put an out of office reply on my messages. Maybe I could get a secretary for my messages from clients in the mean time. I didn't need any more money. I could be set for the rest of my life if I was careful with funds.

I thought about it. Running away from everything and everyone sounded nice. A fresh start. I could change my name and work only when I was bored. Maybe I could become a surf board trainer. Maybe I could just chill out forever.

I saw the water and ocean below us, the land shrinking smaller and smaller. The sparkle of the waves reminded me of our day at the beach. It all reminded me of April. The sooner I left the better. Or at least that was what I kept telling myself. I could never visit that hotel again and I would be fine. It was gorgeous and I would miss it, but I would be fine.

We flew farther and farther away from it as we saw the guy get the girl in the movie. It wasn't a long plane flight from Santa Barbra to Las Vegas, but it felt like it took forever. I couldn't wait for the credits to roll. I couldn't wait to get away from what was the worst weekend of my life.

I never wanted to go to another wedding ever again. I took my phone out and blocked April's number. It was for her own good as well as mine.

25

APRIL

I wiped the sweat off of my brow and clicked my phone to see how much longer I had to run. My heart sank when it saw that I had no new messages. I should have been used to it by now, it had been a week. I was being chased by the wrong guy and ignored by the one I cared about. I pushed harder for the last five minutes and then did the cool down on the treadmill.

Travis was in the tanning room and I was tempted to go break in and cry to him again. I had been more of an emotional wreck now than before I went to the engagement party. I should have seen that coming. No one leaves weddings feeling the same way they did before they went to them, and I was stuck in the worst situation that only got worse as time went on.

I checked the scales. I hadn't lost any more than a pound. Exercising felt useless. I wasn't doing it for fun, and I almost didn't care if I gained all the weight back. I didn't have much hope for a future boyfriend. Getting thinner was the only way I knew to redeem myself, though. So it was what I was going to have to keep doing until I no longer felt so sorry for myself.

It was worse that everyone gave me puppy dog eyes when they saw me. They knew about the wedding. They knew about Tom. When he called off the wedding, everyone was very disappointed and they both blamed me and felt sorry for me. I didn't know what to do. I didn't want Tom back. I never would again. He turned out to be less mature and worthwhile than I remembered.

I wasn't sure what to do at this point. I kept applying for jobs and I kept getting rejections. I could freelance for some money, but I couldn't make a career out of it. I was able to give Travis the money Grant didn't take, but even that didn't cover a fraction of what I owed him.

Travis was being the nicest about this. I think he felt worse since this was sort of his idea. I told him all the details. He agreed that I had a right to be confused about where me and Grant had stood, but he also saw why Grant left.

I didn't blame him either. I drug him along and made him dance like a monkey and he didn't get anything out of it. Tom tried to punch him in the face. I couldn't believe it when I saw it and thinking back made it feel less real. I was going to miss Grant. I shouldn't have gotten my hopes up. Even when he pissed me off, I knew that he had a right to feel the way he did, he wasn't just throwing a fit. Grant had been nice, helping me through what was already a tough weekend. And then, of course, I blew it. I always ruin things that start to go my way.

Travis felt bad and took me out to lunch after the gym. I didn't eat much. I wasn't thinking about food. He kept conversation light. When he noticed that I didn't have much to say in responses he just kept talking about his weekend. He had gotten a call back for an audition. He also told me a crazy story about someone who auditioned beside him. It was funny, but I didn't feel like laughing. I just felt like sulking a little while longer. It wasn't making me feel better, but it was helping me get it out of my system.

When we got back to our place, Travis kept asking me questions. He kept begging for more detail. The more I talked about the weekend, the worse I felt and the more I missed the good times that had happened.

They could have still been happening if I were smart enough to just let Tom be alone.

Tom still tried to call and text me. He did it semi frequently until he finally got the hint. He would leave several messages, and the more he called the drunker he seemed to get. They would have been funny to listen to before but now I just felt bad for the guy. He was spiraling out of control and he had no idea what to do with his life.

Travis saw my glum look when I played the most recent one. "Maybe with his fiancée gone he will be able to focus on work now."

"Let's hope so."

"They can't fire him if his life is falling apart."

"That never stopped him from breaking up with me." We stopped talking again. I deleted the messages.

I hadn't talked to either of my parents yet. I didn't know how. I didn't know what I should say to them. "I told you I shouldn't have gone," was all I could think of, but I didn't even want to say that. I didn't know how much they knew about Grant. I only knew that they knew he had left early. I thought Tom was a decent enough person to keep his mouth shut, but I have been surprised by him time and time again. It was hard to say what he had told everyone.

Tom was back to "Single" on Facebook. He had changed his profile picture, too. He was now single and showing it off. The selfie that was in place now was from before his new girl. I went to Grant's Facebook and flipped through all of the pictures he was tagged in for the third time that week. He had grown so much through the photos. He was so handsome. He didn't have many photos, so it didn't take long to flip through them all. He didn't seem like he actually used his account very much at all. I considered adding him, but if he still wasn't answering my texts I didn't see the point.

Travis left me in the living room while I flipped through them. He stayed in his room for a while and I heard him on the phone. I wondered if Alex knew about this. And if he did, I hope it was through Travis and not through Grant. I didn't like the idea of having a stranger that was so close to my best friend dislike me.

Travis came back in the room and hung up. "That was Alex. I called him to get this for you. Please don't make me regret it." He handed me a piece of paper with an address on it. It was in Vegas.

"Is this real?"

"Yes. He lives in the penthouse of this building. If you get a restraining order, I don't know how much more help I can be. Just be… careful. Use your best discretion." I hugged Travis tight and put the paper in my pocket.

"You should probably pack a bag. Just in case."

It took about 5 hours to get to Vegas so I left immediately. It was hardly noon. If I budgeted time right, I could get there in four hours. I didn't know his schedule, or if he was even home for that matter but I didn't care. I could drive back the next day and the day after that until I saw him.

I wanted to take Travis with me. Going on an adventure like this alone was frightening. I hadn't done something like this ever before and now was a very emotional time for me. I stocked up on all the road trip necessities like gummy worms and energy drinks. I put in a Blonde CD and began the journey.

The car ride went fast. Too fast. I had memorized a monologue for an apology over and over again in my head, but I still felt like I didn't have enough time to prepare. I had never been to Vegas before, so when I pulled through it was a culture shock. I saw all the signs on the buildings. This place had to be lit up at night almost as well as it was during the day time. There were people everywhere, scrambling from casino to casino. You could tell by the cars on the street where the good and bad neighborhoods were.

I grew more anxious the closer I got to my destination. When I went through a gated community, I was worried I went too far. I was in the right area though. As I pulled up to the largest, most lavish hotel in the area it began to sink in just how much he was worth. It was all Egyptian themed. The entire building looked like it was made of gold. Even the parking lot was paved with shinning bricks. I felt nauseous as I walked closer. I didn't belong. This was all a mistake.

I didn't drive across state for nothing, though. No matter how badly I wanted to turn around, I knew I couldn't. Even if this was the last time that I ever stepped foot in Vegas, I knew that I had to do what I came to do.

26

GRANT

My doorbell rang while I was in the middle of packing the last of my things. I had finally decided to go on a small vacation. Okay, a big vacation. I thought that Australia would be a good place. I heard only good things about it. Hawaii was on the list too, but I was getting a bit disenchanted with it by the amount of times that I have visited it on business. I didn't know how long I wanted to be gone either. I know I wanted to leave long enough to get a break from everyone and everything, but I wanted to be back in time to see my half brother be born.

Thinking about it made my skin crawl. I wasn't going to be the youngest anymore. I would have none of the privileges with all of the down side. This was sure to take some of my dad's attention off of me, but it would just make my mom that much more desperate for all her kids. If I had kids, they would have an uncle that was only a few years their elder. I hated the thought.

It took me a bit to sort through the things of mine that were by the door to get to it. I didn't bother looking through the peephole. I would regret that.

It was her outside my door. I had no idea what to do when I saw her there, standing outside. I began to shut the door again and I groaned with it.

"Wait!" she said. She pushed the door and let herself in. I plopped down on my coach and I waited for her to talk until she was done bothering me. She followed me to the coach and sat beside me. "Let me just talk to you. It won't take long."

I said nothing. I walked further into my house. She followed. I was starting to regret not locking my door. I would always check the peephole from now on.

"Talking to me is the least you could do after ignoring all my calls and texts. Besides, driving here by myself is probably the boldest thing I have and will ever do so this is your one chance to hear me out."

I turned back to look at her. She followed me everywhere I went. I should have gone on vacation the minute I got back. I decided there was no more point, and I went back to the coach. I would be gone soon. I laid with my face down.

"You have five minutes. Anymore, and you won't be able to afford me."

She sounded annoyed. I might have hurt her by saying that. "Ouch, okay. That's mean. But fine."

"Time starts now."

"Okay, so originally when we went away, I was using you. And what I wanted to happen happened exactly." She wasn't helping herself. I considered cutting her time short. "But that isn't what I wanted after all. When you saw me downstairs with Tom, I'll be honest, he came on to me. He said he missed me. He said that he wanted what we have and I couldn't let him think that. I didn't want him to miss me anymore. I just wanted to be done with him. And now I am done with him, but I don't have you anymore."

I turned my head to look at her while she spoke. She picked at her nails, but she looked me in the eyes with sincerity. I thought about the drive from her place to here. It had to have taken at least 4 hours. I didn't know how she got my address. I didn't care at this point. I just wanted to hear what she had to say until there was peace in the world again. "Keep talking."

"So, when we went away, I was already confused. I have had an awful two years, and just when I think that my life can't get worse, it does. But then, with you, I was having a really great time. I didn't worry about the next day, and I didn't worry about the day before. You made me feel like I didn't have anything to worry about at all. It was so easy to hang out with you."

It had been easy to get to know her. I still didn't want to talk to her. She made me feel used. I knew that that had been my job, and it was my fault for being emotional, but I didn't think that she would have been the type of person that took advantage of another person like that.

"The whole time I was getting to know you, it seemed like we spent most of that in front of other people, so it was hard to tell if you were acting or not. And then we had that dumb fight, and I knew you weren't acting. I knew that maybe we did have something after all. I was pretty sold. I don't know why I decided to listen to Tom. I was going to tell him off. I didn't even let him talk me into seeing him again. He has been calling me nonstop all week, and I haven't answered him once. That is so unlike me. When he and I were together I would wait on him hand and foot, and now I see him groveling and begging for me to come back. The only difference is that now that I have seen him, I don't feel that way anymore. He wants me, but I don't want him."

I was starting to get frustrated. I had heard enough about Tom in the past two weeks for me to write a novel on how big of an asshole he was. It made me think back to that morning. I checked all around the room for her. I looked out on the balcony, even, and she wasn't there. When she didn't come back with breakfast I started to worry. I went down. I was betrayed. She hadn't done anything wrong, but she didn't do anything right either. "Well, what exactly do you want, April? It seems like you and Tom are both confused by each other and you're taking down other people in the process. If you know you don't want him so bad then tell me, what is it that you do want?"

I sat on the edge of the couch, staring at her. My breathing had come erratic and I wanted to disappear. I didn't want her to come visit me. I didn't want to see her. I didn't want her to know how much she effected me, how much she hurt me. She looked back to me. I saw the sadness in her eyes. I had no idea I meant anything to her.

I could feel her starting to lose her patience. I asked again. "Tell me, what do you want?" This time I said it softer. I crossed my fingers and prayed for the best. My wish came true.

"You."

27

APRIL

I couldn't believe those words came out of my mouth. I had gotten caught up in the heat of the moment again. Again, I wanted to take the words back, scooping them into my mouth and swallowing them like a magic trick. I didn't babble over it this time. I just looked back at him.

I had shocked myself, and I could tell that my answer shocked him too. After the silence filled the air for a few moments, I saw a smile spread across his face. I became nervous. Had I used the right combination of words? Did I win him back?

I didn't know what to say, and I wasn't sure why he wasn't saying anything either. I had laid all I had on the table. I drove over 5 hours to get here to apologize, and now I wasn't sure he deserved or wanted an apology. I still wanted him. It was true. He was what I wanted.

If I could go back and time and change it so that I never went to the lobby to meet Tom, I would have. If I could have just stayed in bed and kept my eyes and mouth shut, I would have. It was too late now. I messed up again. He didn't have to date me in the first place, he certainly wasn't going to after I hurt him.

Grant had called it, though. I don't know if he had a premonition or just experience, but he had known from the beginning we were going to have sex. Maybe it happened because he said it would. Maybe it happened because I actually wanted it to, too. Even when I looked at him now, I still wanted him.

I noticed the suitcases around the room. The furniture stayed here, but it looked like most of the things around here were being moved. The inside was just as fancy as the outside. His place was well furnished and finished, even when it was bare of all decorations. Was I too late? How long had he known he was going to be moving? He never mentioned it to me before. I guess we really never talked about much before.

I wanted to know him better, though. I wanted to be able to tell everyone his favorite movie, his pet peeves, and I wanted to know his birthday. I wanted to know if his family was as crazy as mine, and I wanted to know about what he has been doing the past 27 years. But I wasn't going to be able to learn anything new because I blew it. Even when I didn't do anything, I still messed things up. I was just a walking wreck. He was smarter for avoiding me. I saw that now.

A few more silent moments went by and I stood to leave. I didn't want to stand here and be mocked by him. I had had enough damage in the past week to need to buy a new life. If he could be an escort, maybe I could too. It would get my parents off my back about money, for sure. It might even get Tom off my back for good. I clearly didn't know what to say or do to win him back, so I was going to have to give up my dream. I turned and walked to the door. I had never done anything that soul baring before and it still didn't work out for me.

"Wait." I stopped and turned around. He was standing up, but wasn't looking at me. He looked at his nails and began to pick them. That was my nervous habit, too. "I don't know if you can have me."

I looked at the boxes again. I wasn't sure if he meant that in an escort way, or a timely since. Maybe neither. Maybe he thought he couldn't handle me. He was starting to get on my nerves. "Is it because you don't think I can take it?"

"No. It's because I know I can't." He smiled at me when he said it. I felt my heart flutter. Was he beginning to flirt with me again, or was I just getting my hopes up?

"That's too bad for you." I flirted back, inching my way back into his apartment. "Because I wasn't going to hurt you. I just wanted to have a little piece of you."

"Just a little piece, huh?" He walked closer towards me too, moving as slowly as I was. He walked with meaning, but he was very playful when he did it. "How big of a piece is that?"

"Oh, I don't know. If you can't handle it then, I understand. All I really wanted from you was one measly date. That's all."

"That's all?"

"Yep."

"You aren't going to tear me apart, or force me to go to another engagement party?"

I giggled. "Nope. I was just hoping to maybe go get some dinner with you. I have never been to Vegas before. But I see that that might be too much for your little heart."

"My heart? So you aren't using me as an escort Grant? You aren't just trying to get me to chaperone you around the city?"

"Nope. Just trying to get you to go one a date, as date Grant and date April."

"And there is no business arrangements? You won't pay me for holding your hand or anything like that?"

"I won't pay you a cent. I couldn't if I wanted to."

"Good." He smiled and we were inches away. "Because you're awful at business arrangements."

"I know." I was pressed up against his body and I could feel his abs through his shirt. "I'm no businessman like you."

He quieted me with his lips. It had been too long since we had last kissed. I felt the butterflies be release more and more in my stomach, being sent out by the thousands. The way he moved his lips in mine made my legs turn to jelly. My heart was weak for him. I couldn't have pushed him away if I had wanted to, and I knew I never would have.

He kissed me again and again, moving to my neck. He was beginning to make me gasp. I put my hands around his shoulders. He moved back up to my face and gave me one final kiss.

"So then how do you feel about sushi?"

"I love it."

"Because," his eyebrows perked and he looked mischievous, "we could just stay inside tonight, if you really want to."

"As tempting as that offer is, I have never been to the city, and as soon as you said the word sushi my mouth began to water."

"Sushi it is. But I'm paying this time." He grabbed his billfold and stuffed it in his pocket.

"I wouldn't have it any other way."

THE END

DEAR READER

Enjoyed reading Book One of *The Arrangement*? Can't wait to find out what happens next?

You can get a FREE (Gifted) copy of Part One of The Arrangement Book Two!

Just leave an honest review of Book One at the retailer where it was downloaded. Then send us a screenshot of the review including the title of the book and the name of the retailer where it was downloaded to us at contact@charlotte-byrd.com

Also, please mention that you want to the FREE copy of Part One of The Arrangement Book 2.

Thanks for reading!

Love,

Charlotte Byrd

FREE EXCERPT: THE DEBT

When Brielle Thompson, a 25-year-old waitress, receives a mysterious check for $250,000, she uses the money to pay for her mother's very expensive cancer treatment, saving her life.

Two years later, she is called to pay back her debt. All she has to do is travel to an isolated mansion and work for one year as a personal assistant to an arrogant asshole whom she hates.

Wyatt Wild is a **gorgeous alpha billionaire playboy who's not used to girls saying no to him**. He has bedded models, actresses and socialites and then a waitress from some crappy roadside café dares reject him. Who does she think she is?

Wyatt always gets what he wants and his desires focus on the innocent and stubborn Brielle .

Neither give in easily and they quickly get locked in a **game of seduction.**

Hot, Steamy and Romantic!

1

WYATT

I wanted to fuck her the first time I saw her. She wasn't my type. Not at all. A little plump with messy brown hair, and a sweaty forehead from taking too many orders and delivering food to strangers who left her fifty cent tips.

She was dressed in a plain white t-shirt and ratty jeans. The jeans dragged a bit on the floor, and the holes were definitely not made by a manufacturer. No respectable girl I knew would ever wear something like that and that made me want her even more.

Her jeans were tight at the waist, and she adjusted them periodically. Pulling them up over her hips while pulling down her shirt. She was trying to hide her figure as if she was embarrassed by her gorgeous thighs, hips, and breasts. Contemporary society is all fucked up. This girl's, this woman's body, was what every man wants. Every straight man of every race, ethnicity and creed. A tiny waist, shapely hips and legs, and breasts big enough to grab on to. Despite that, all the women's magazines try to do is to convince them that they're too fat because they're not shaped like 12-year-old boys!

The name tag on her shirt said, Brielle, which was a fancy French name to have for a girl who worked at a crappy roadside diner in the middle of the workday. It didn't take a genius to figure out that this was her full-time job. I would be surprised if she worked here to get through school. There wasn't a college for a hundred miles in any direction.

No, this Brielle was all wrong for me. And the worst part was that she didn't have any money!

I don't like girls without money. It's not because I'm shallow. It's because I'm practical. I don't fuck girls without money because it gets too complicated. It's much more likely to make things more complicated. Girls without money feel taken advantage of. They want to see me more. They think that a one night stand is unreasonable. And if it goes past one or two nights then they want me to save them. Rescue them from their pathetic little lives. But I'm not a prince. I'm not a white knight either. I don't have it in me even though I do own a white horse that I love to ride.

I don't like to rescue girls. I don't like needy girls. No, the girls I fuck have to have their own careers – a starring role in a TV show, a signed contract with a prominent modeling agency, or at the very least a reasonably-sized trust fund with one or two million from mommy and daddy. Oh hell, who are we kidding? It's always from daddy.

I established these rules long ago. And I abide by them religiously. They are there to keep both of us safe. To make sure that we both have fun, but not too much. I don't want the girls I fuck to have expectations about me. Expectations that I will never live up to.

And now, walking into this café, and seeing Brielle, I'm ready to toss them out of the window. I want her. I want to put my throbbing cock in her wet pussy and pull her hair until she moans.

I got hard in anticipation as I watch her take an order from an old trucker at the next table.

"Hey, what the hell do you think you're doing?" Brielle says, pushing his hand away from her ass.

I was too focused on her breasts that I hadn't even noticed the trucker's itchy hand reach out and grab her ass.

"Oh I'm so sorry," he says sarcastically and laughs to his friend.

"Not as sorry as you're going to be," she says, grabbing his uneaten plate of food.

"What the hell are you doing?"

"I don't know where you think you are, but this isn't *that* kind of establishment. You can't just go around touching women inappropriately here. And you'd better get the hell out."

"But I didn't finish eating," the trucker stands up dumbfounded. He reaches out for his plate, but she moves it away from him.

"You're done," she says with the kind of determination in her voice that makes me ever more hard.

"Please leave," Brielle says. "And don't come back."

"I'd like to see your manager, you little cunt. You're going to get fired."

"I'm the manager here. Now, get the fuck out!"

I get out of the booth and stand next to her. I'm thankful for my loose fitting jeans.

"You heard her, sir," I say. "The lady would like you to leave. So please leave."

People at the next booths start to clap, and cheer and my friends join in. The trucker and his friend curse her out, but head toward the door.

"You're a real cunt. You know that? You're going to be sorry for this!"

I'm standing right next to her and, though, she's trying to stay strong, I can see that she's really shaken. Her chest is flushed, and the trucker's plate is rattling slightly in her hand.

"That was really impressive," I say.

She turns to me.

"I'm probably going to get fired over it."

"I thought you were the manager?"

"No," she shakes her head and starts to gather the plates and cutlery from the trucker's booth. "The manager's coming in later tonight. I'm just the waitress."

"Well, I don't see why you'd get fired. He had no right to grab your ass like that. He was a real asshole."

"Thanks," she smiles. Her smile lights up the room. "Can I get that in writing from you?"

"Yes, of course."

I startle her. Catch her off- guard, in a good way. I like that.

"I'm just kidding," she finally says. "Let me just get all this stuff to the kitchen and I'll come back and take your order."

When I return to the booth, the guys laugh and slap me on the shoulders. They know she's not my type, they know that I'm breaking my rules.

"I don't know, Tyler. Looks like Wyatt's in love," Logan laughs.

"With a waitress!" Tyler chimes in.

"What happened to only dating girls with jobs or rich girls? Preferably both?" Ryan asks.

"She's got a job," I say. "We're at her job."

"Oh, please. A waitress? That's not a real job. You're breaking your rules, and you know it," Logan jokes.

It's all in good fun, but right now I hate their teasing. They're right of course, and still I want her.

"Nothing's happening. I don't know what you're talking about," I say as assertively as possible.

"We see the way you're looking at her," Ryan says. "We're not blind."

"I was just impressed with what she did. Brielle's got spunk."

"Oh, Brielle, is it? You two are on first names basis already?" Tyler chuckles. Dammit. I shouldn't have let that slip.

"It's on her fuckin' name tag, idiot," I try to save myself. But they're not buying it.

Brielle comes back to our table to take our order. After writing down everyone else's orders, she looks up at me from her notepad. My cock gets hard again, and I push it back down, under the table.

"You know, you made quite an impression on our friend, Wyatt, here," Logan suddenly says.

"Is that so?"

"I really liked how you handled that trucker," I say. I feel like I'm on my back foot. I don't like coming on to girls in this manner. I glare at Logan, but he doesn't stop.

"Wyatt was just telling us that you're not at all like the girls we're used to," Logan continues.

"Well, working for a living would do that to you," she says with a smile. I hate how she mocks me for having money. I want her even more now. I want to push her down on the bed, and I want her to let me tie her hands to the bedpost. I want to tease her until she screams my name.

"So what would you like? Wyatt, is it?" she turns to me.

I had picked out something on the menu, but now I couldn't remember what it was.

"What would you recommend, Brielle?" I say reading her name tag. Her name is burned on my cock, but I can't let her know that. Not yet.

"Our spinach omelet with feta cheese is quite good."

"Okay, I'll take that."

THE CAFÉ CLEARS OUT A BIT. While my friends continue to pick at their food, I excuse myself and head toward the bathroom. Before I get there, I pop into the back and find Brielle sitting on a crate reading a book. She quickly puts it away, but not before I catch the title. Jane Eyre. My sister's favorite.

"Can I help you with something?"

"No, not really."

She stares at me. I know I need a reason for being here.

"Yes, actually. I was just wondering if I can take you out for a drink sometime."

I catch her off guard. Her face lights up, and a brief smile crosses her face.

"That's probably not a good idea," she says with a forlorn sigh.

"Why's that?"

"Well, for one thing, you don't even live here."

"How do you know?" I ask.

She furrows her brows and folds her arms across her chest, pressing her breasts together in front of me. They look as if they are on a platter, and it requires all the strength within me not to reach out and touch them.

"People who drive Bentleys don't live around here."

She's right, of course.

"And the other thing?"

She takes a deep breath.

"I'm not looking for a relationship."

"Who said anything about a relationship?" I ask and immediately regret my choice of words.

"And I'm definitely not looking for anything casual."

"Why's that?" I ask.

I should just drop it, but I can't. No one, and I mean, *no one* has ever turned me down. I can't even believe that this is really happening. Maybe she's just toying with me. Maybe she's just flirting.

"Because I'm not into one night stands, Wyatt," she says and walks away. I love the sound of my name in her mouth. I want to put more of me there.

Brielle avoided eye contact with me the rest of the time that we were there. That made me want her even more. She was feisty, and hot and she didn't take shit from anyone. An unusual girl. I wanted her so much I thought I was going to explode.

When she came over with the check, I purposely extended my hand. She tried to place the plastic cover with the check into my hand, but I took the opportunity to reach out and touch her. Her touch was electric. It sent shivers through my body.

Suddenly, Brielle let go of the plastic cover, and it dropped to the floor.

"I'm sorry," she said. "I'm so clumsy."

"No, I'm the one who's sorry." I apologized.

I could hear Logan, Tyler and Ryan smirking at me from around the table. But my eyes remained fixed on Brielle. When she bent over, her cleavage expanded, and her breasts looked like they were going to spill out of her t-shirt.

"Thank you," I say and hand Logan the check.

It was Logan's turn to cover the bill. We never split the bill, unless it was a VIP table at a Vegas nightclub or something extravagant like that. The bill at this roadside café hardly registered as real money. Logan's family was equally wealthy, but he was cheap on tips.

If the girl didn't flirt with him or go really out of her way to impress him, he didn't like to leave her more than fifteen percent.

I made sure that I was the last one out of the booth and quickly slipped a $100 bill under the check.

2

BRIELLE

I notice him just as he pulled into our little dusty parking lot with his Bentley. That car costs more money than I'll make in a decade. There are five guys in it, all equally attractive and cocky, but he was the only one who caught my attention.

Tall, handsome, tan. Blue eyes and dark sandy hair that made him look like a brooding dark stranger and a surfer boy depending on the light.

He strolled into my café with a confident and laid back swagger that would make male models jealous. There's a carefree nature to his demeanor and yet, at the same time, there's something very intense about him.

I like the way that he says my name. I like the way that he's impressed with my ability to deal with annoying pestering old men. What he doesn't know is that, unfortunately, I'm used to unwanted sexual advances from gross strangers. What that trucker did was one of the least offensive things, frankly. The men who come in the middle of the night try worse things.

Wyatt wants to take me out for a drink. Yes, yes, yes, I say to myself. Say yes. You deserve this. But I reject him. I want to say yes, more than anything, but I can't. I'm too fragile to have my heart broken by the likes of him. And, of course, it would happen. He's cocky and rich and arrogant, and guys like that only want one thing. The thing that I certainly want to have with him, but not now. Not considering everything else I have that's going on.

THE FOLLOWING DAY, just as the sun throws its harshest rays on our dusty part of the world, my mind drifts back to Wyatt. If only he would walk back into this place. If only he would ask me again. Then maybe I would say yes. But it's all a daydream.

My mind drifts from one part of his body to another. He's got the kind of veins lining his forearms that make me wet in my panties. I want to pull off that $200 t-shirt and run my fingers over his chiseled abs. I want to grab both of his butt cheeks at the same time and get down on my knees before him.

"Brielle?"

A familiar voice startles me and brings me back down to earth. It's Wyatt. He's casually leaning on the countertop and tapping his fingers.

"Hey," he says.

"Hey."

I'm at a loss for words. My mouth gets parched.

"So I was in the neighborhood, and I thought I'd stop by."

"Oh, okay," I smile. "Can I get you a menu."

"You can, but I'll just get whatever you recommend anyway."

His cockiness is oozing out of him. I look around. His friends are nowhere to be found. But the Bentley is parked in the first available non-handicapped parking spot.

"Where are your friends?" I ask.

"Not here," he smiles.

"Why are you?"

He takes a breath. "Like I said, I was passing through the neighborhood."

I roll my eyes.

"You don't believe me?"

"No," I shake my head. This guy is dangerous. In a good way. No, in a bad way.

"Well, take a seat. Anywhere you want," I say.

He looks around the café. There are three other people here. The lunch 'rush' just left, meaning the four other people who typically pop in for lunch. Wyatt chooses the seat at the counter. Right in front of me.

I grab a rag to pick up the few crumbs left over by the last customer and notice that my book is still in my hand.

"Jane Eyre," he nods. I hide the book behind the counter and wipe the counter around him. He doesn't move his arms, and I stop to see if he will. He takes a moment before lifting his arms.

"You were reading that yesterday," he says. I nod and get my pad out. I can't find my pen and frantically look for it at the cash register. I can feel his gazing burning a hole in the back of my jeans. He's checking out my ass. I don't want to admit it, but I like it. A lot.

"Yes, I'm not done yet. Have you read it?"

"Yes, in school. It's got a good story. Love and tension. Lots of awkward situations,

It just needs something."

"You think a classic of English literature needs something? Seriously?" My tongue often gets away from me, but this is one of those situations where I don't really care. I love talking about literature, and he was the one who brought it up.

"Yes, so what?" he shrugs.

I shake my head at his arrogance. He's an asshole, and he knows it. He also knows that in some situations, like this one, it's ridiculously hot.

"So what does Jane Eyre need? How would you improve on Emily Bronte's masterpiece?"

"Hey, I'm not saying it's bad. I'm just saying that it's missing something that would really make it complete."

I cross my arms over my chest and wait for him to answer my question. This should be good!

"It needs sex. Lots of sex."

I stare at him.

"They have so much sexual tension. They are cooped up in this house together. They have all of these feelings developing for one another. We as the audience need a release. We need them to have sex. And lots of it."

I can hardly believe what I'm hearing.

"That's crazy," I shake my head. "Jane Eyre doesn't need sex."

"Oh yes, she does. C'mon, aren't you just aching to read about them doing it?"

"Doing it? In Jane Eyre? Tempting, but no," I say definitively. How crude and vulgar and insulting can he be?

"Okay, it doesn't have to actually use those words. It can be much more poetic than that. But still as graphic."

"Like what, for example?"

He takes a moment to think about it. I wonder if he's going to choose a metaphor or go straight for a direct and honest description.

"How about this?" Wyatt leans back from the counter tilting his head back. He lifts up his hand in the pose I've only seen professors do in movies.

"He slid his big cock into that heavenly place between her legs."

The words dangle in the air between us as if they are suspended by a string. I don't say anything for a moment. I'm speechless. I want to be embarrassed, but I'm more turned on than anything.

"So both graphic and romantic is your suggestion?" I finally say.

He nods. "I thought that struck an interesting tension between the two depicting both his masculinity and her femininity in just the right way."

I smile and blush. I think so, too.

"You know you can't really talk like this in a public place," I say.

"Well, I'd love to go somewhere private," he leans closer to me.

His confidence is exuberant. I want to say yes. More than anything I want to say, yes. I want him to take me somewhere private and have his way with me.

"I'm sorry," I start.

"Awe, why?" he leans even closer and runs his fingers over my hand. I want to grab it and pull him close to me. I want to kiss his luscious lips and suck his tongue into my mouth.

But I pull my hand away.

"I just can't, not now."

"When? Why?" At that moment, Wyatt's deep set eyes resemble those I've seen in photographs of the Great Depression. Lost. Forgotten. Broken.

I can't explain. He's a stranger. And I feel like if I say *it* out loud to someone, I will burst out crying and never stop.

3

WYATT

Her words pierce through my heart. Now, I want her even more. I thought that things would be different since I came alone. I left my friends back home and drove two hours back to this god-forsaken town to see her again. She doesn't know this, of course. I hate the feelings of helplessness that she evokes in me. Why? Why didn't she say yes this time?

I have to have her. Not against her will. I have to make her beg for me.

I look at Brielle. She stares at me with a blank stare that's impossible to read. She brings me my food and disappears back into the kitchen. She's not staying around to talk. I have no reason to eat at this shitty place without her presence.

"Don't take it personally," an older woman with a lifelong smoker's voice says.

She has been sitting at the far end of the counter all this time, but I didn't notice her until now. The woman came closer. She smells of cigarettes and wears a small white apron with pockets, just like Brielle. There's no dress code here, but I know she's a waitress. Her name tag is old, and worn and I can't read her name.

"Brielle's going through a lot right now."

I nod as if I understand. The old woman is thin but looks as strong as an ox. She leans over the counter.

"Brielle just doesn't want more complications in her life right now," she whispers.

"What do you mean?"

"You know about her mom, right?"

"Yes," I lie.

"Well, she's getting worse. Neither of them can afford the chemo treatments anymore, and the insurance ran out a few months ago. It's looking really grim."

I nod. Her mom's dying of cancer.

"There's some experimental procedure that's available and looks like it could be an excellent option for her."

"That's good," I say.

"Yeah, except that Brielle can't afford it. She can't even come close."

"How much does it cost?"

"Not sure. Thousands. A couple hundred or so, I heard. And who's got that kind of money?"

I look away. My gaze drifts outside to my Bentley. That car costs as much as a cancer treatment to save someone's life. I've never put it in that perspective before.

The old woman startles me when she puts her long shriveled up fingers on my face and turns it toward her.

"So don't take it personally, kid. She's got a lot on her mind. But I know she likes you. I saw the way she was looking at you. In the seven years that I've known her, I've never seen her look like that at a guy before."

4

BRIELLE

I've entered the double- wide trailer, which has been my home since I was six, with a sense of dread. My Momma's hospital bed barely fits into the back room and ever since we had that installed everything else had to be moved around and put into every which crevice throughout the house it would fit in. Clothes and boxes and shoes and magazines are everywhere. Now that Momma's not working at the bar, I have to work twice as many hours just to make the same amount of money. And it's never enough.

She has to take more and more pills, and the prices are constantly changing. Last month, one of her pills costs $40 for a week supply, and now it's $325 for the same amount, without much of explanation as to why. I empty my pockets. The tips from the regulars after an 8-hour shift are a little over $12. I don't blame them.

They don't have much to spare themselves. But it's not enough. Not nearly enough.

I reach into my other pocket and pull out a crisp $100 bill. Wyatt left it before I could come back and stop him. He left me a $100 tip yesterday, too. I'm eternally grateful. These $200 will go a long way in paying this month's rent and the rest of the bills. Might even let me get some of my mom's jewelry from that pawn shop. No, I can't think like that. Medication is more important than heirlooms.

"Is that you, Brielle?" I hate how faint my Momma's voice is. She used to be such a tough and strong woman. She never took shit from anyone, especially not the men. I'm much shyer and unsure of myself than she is. Not as confident. Not as strong. But now, my Momma is weak and tired.

"Don't come in yet," she says when I approach the door.

"Momma, it's okay," I say through the door. I hear her moving around in the bed and making a ruckus. Things are falling over and a glass shatters.

"Shit, shit, shit," she says. I'm about to open the door.

"Don't you dare open that door, Brielle Elizabeth Cole."

When Momma uses my full name, I know she really means it.

After a couple more minutes, she shouts, "Okay, I'm ready."

I walk in. She's looking into her compact and adjusting her wig. Her face is made up to the ten. Her eyebrows are penciled in, and she's even wearing fake eyelashes. She finishes off the look with a generous slather of lipstick and smiles at me.

"You look beautiful," I say trying to hold back tears.

"Oh, C'mon, don't start now. If you cry, you'll make me cry and then all this work will go to hell."

I smile. I love my Momma's soft Southern accent. She was born in Kentucky and moved to California when she was sixteen with her first husband, but her accent never went away.

"What would you like for dinner?" I ask trying to change the subject. Momma looks like she's ready to go to a ball, but all we will be doing is sitting around the television with tray tables and eating whatever concoction I dream up.

"Macaroni and cheese?" she asks.

"Again?" We've had it for a week straight.

"I'm afraid it's the only thing I can keep down nowadays."

I nod and head to the kitchen. When I get the butter out, tears are flowing out of my eyes uncontrollably, and I can't stop them.

Momma worked hard all of her life. She's worked since the age of fourteen, and she deserves better than this. She's only 44 years old, for goodness sake! And now she's dying a slow and horrible death. She can't eat anything without throwing it up again. The chemo is poisoning her, and we can't even afford the poison anymore. And there's nothing I can do to stop any of this.

A week later

I am driving home from work on a beautiful, sunny day, thinking that the sky is so blue and, there's not a single cloud as far as the eye can see. My legs are cramping up, and I can't wait to get home to climb into bed. I'm not much of a morning person and these morning shifts are killing me.

I worked from 4 am until noon, and this eight-hour shift was harder than the busy evenings shifts any day. Barely anyone comes in after ten and breakfast customers don't like to tips as much as dinner customers.

I finally pull onto our street and see the house in the distance. The paint is peeling on the side, and the porch is cluttered with junk, which we no longer have room for inside the house. I need to take care of that one of these days. Just don't know how or when. Paint costs money. Putting junk away doesn't, but I don't know where to put it. A shed is close to $1000 and I'm not going to have that kind of money anytime soon. Cardboard boxes? Perhaps. But boxes full of junk are easier to steal than loose junk.

The street leading up to the house isn't really a street, but a dirt road. When we first moved here and Momma's second husband, my father, was still around, we would wash the car every week. Within a day, the desert's dry climate and our dirt road would deposit a thin layer of dust on the car making the exercise fruitless. My father insisted that we had to do it because of pride. But he left by the time I turned eight and took the car. I guess his pride extended only to the car, not to his family. We didn't have another car for more than a year after that.

I pull up to the chain linked gate and get out. The neighbor's pit bull and Rottweiler are already going nuts. They welcome me home from work multiple times a day with the excitement of a full marching band and always put a smile on my face.

"Hey, Bella. Boomer," I wave to them. "I'll be right over."

I put the car in park, get out and pull the gate open. I get back in the car, park and head over to the dogs. The other neighbors are afraid of them, but they are the sweetest dogs I've ever met. I stick my hands through the chain linked fence and pet them each on their heads.

After the brief hello, which is honestly, the highlight of my day, I try to pull the gate closed before heading in. Usually, this is barely a process at all. But today, the wheels on the bottom, which squeak so loudly they send shivers up my spine, get stuck. When I pull them harder, they take off and run over my foot.

"Shit, shit, shit," I curse hopping on one foot. "Dammit."

The gate needs to be oiled, but I don't really have any extra money to spend on WD-40 or the time to drive out to Home Depot to get it.

"Stupid gate!" I kick it, instead. Not a great solution.

I'm about to head inside when, out of the corner of my eye, I see the mail truck. I am about to turn back, but something keeps me there. Getting the mail is not as exciting of an event as it once was. A long time ago, I remembered looking forward to getting cards in the mail from my grandparents and tearing through envelopes with the words "Sweepstakes" and "Winner" on the cover. But nowadays, the only thing that comes in the mail is medical bills.

Despite that, something is holding me back. I wait for the mail truck to pull next to the house. The mailman is a sweet old man who has been delivering mail for close to thirty years or so. Whenever we are short on money, and I have to say that the check is in the mail, even though it isn't, I've always felt bad about it because I know that I'm blaming it on him.

"How's your mom?" he asks. There's no way to really answer that question. Throwing up every morning, afternoon and night. Staying in bed all day long. People don't want to hear these things.

"Hanging in there," I say. It's the best way to describe the teetering that she's doing between this world and the next.

The mailman hands me a thick stack of envelopes. All are approximately the same size, and I know they're all bills. I sigh and head to the house.

I don't have any money to pay any of the bills I will have to spend days in the coming week on the phone talking with various administrators at the hospital and Momma's different doctors' offices all with the hopes of getting some of the bills reduced.

I toss the pile of bills on the kitchen table and open the refrigerator door looking for something to eat. I've been up since 3:30 am so a simple grilled cheese sandwich is a no- brainer. While the skillet is heating up, I check on Momma, who's fast asleep with the blinds still down.

When I sit down at the kitchen table, I reach for the remote to flip on the TV and accidentally knock the stack of bills onto the floor.

"Dammit," I say. I gather all the envelopes, but one stands out. It's different than the rest, and my name is written on it in a beautiful cursive script.

Ms. Brielle Elizabeth Cole

I look at the envelope closer. The paper is fancier than the others. And the stamp is unusual not the standard issue stamps that they sell at the post office. It has a detailed painting of a buffalo in a field of grass.

There's no return address in the upper left- hand corner. When I turn the envelope around, I see that it's from The Wild Foundation. Something about that name sounds familiar. Wild. What's Wild? Is it Wild International, the pharmaceutical company?

Instead of tearing the envelope open like I usually do, I get a knife and carefully slice open the top.

Dear Ms. Brielle Elizabeth Cole,
It has come to our attention that your mother is gravely ill. Please use the following check to pay for her treatment.

There's more to the letter, but that's the only part I see. I read it over and over, not believing my eyes. I look into the envelope again and pull out a check.

$250,000

The check is for a quarter of a million dollars! I don't believe it. This must be some sort of fake. A joke. But why? Who would do this? Why would someone play a joke on me like this?

When Momma wakes up, I show her the check and the letter.

"I've seen this on Dr. Phil, Brielle. Don't cash it. It's from some scammer. A love scam."

"But you gotta be talking to someone for them to send you a check like this, don't you?"

"Who have you been talking to?" she asks furrowing her brows.

"No one! All I do is go to work and take you to doctors appointments. I don't have any time to waste talking to strangers."

Momma tells me to throw the check away, but I don't listen. Instead, I stay up late after my evening shift and go online. I look up Wild International. It's a big pharmaceutical company, which has just gone public. It's owned by some cute young guy named Gatsby Wild. Why the hell his parents would name him after someone so tragic is beyond me!

The next morning, I look up the Wild Foundation on my phone and call them. A pleasant young woman answers and confirms that the foundation does indeed exist, and they're located in Los Angeles.

"So are you in the habit of mailing out large checks to strangers?" I ask. I don't mean to be rude or direct, but I don't know how else to go about finding out if this is indeed a real check.

"Ms. Cole, that's primarily all we do," she says.

I'm dumbfounded. I explain my situation to her and wait for her laugh at me in my face. But she doesn't.

"I can always check your name in our database. And make sure that this is a legit check that came from us."

"Yes, please, do that."

She asks me to wait on the phone and puts me on hold. I don't wait too long, but the few minutes that do pass feels like it takes a century to expire.

I put on the teapot to pass the time. I also find one of the last tea bags at the back of the cupboard and make a note to buy more.

"Ms. Cole?" she says. I can barely hear her over the boiling water in the teapot, and I quickly shut it off.

"Yes, I'm here."

"I've got good news for you. Your name is on the list of approved donations and I also double checked whether a check was actually issued to you and I see that it was issued five days ago."

I can't respond. I've lost the ability to speak.

"Ms. Cole? Are you there?" she asks. Louder this time.

"Yes, yes, I'm here," I mumble. "So it's okay? I can cash the check?"

"Yes, please do. And if the bank gives you any trouble, just tell them to call this number."

She dictates the number of her boss, and I write it down on the back of the envelope.

When I get off the phone, I don't know if I'm going to cry or laugh. I feel like I could do either. Tears start streaming down my face, and I call for Momma. She's still asleep, but I don't care. We have the money to pay for her treatment. Whatever treatment she needs. My whole body begins to shake, and both my hands and feet go numb.

"Oh my god, Brielle? What's wrong?" Momma comes out of her room and slowly makes her way to me.

"What happened? What's wrong?"

She wraps her arms around me and begins to rock me from side to side. Tears continue to run down my face, but they are not tears of sorrow. I just can't catch my breath long enough to tell her.

"It's going to be okay, baby girl. Whatever it is, we'll get through it."

Suddenly, I start to laugh. "Yes, yes, it is," I say hugging her back.

"It's going to be more than okay, Momma."

"What are you talking about?"

"I just got off the phone with the Wild Foundation and the check's legit. They're paying for your treatment. You're going to get some real help now, Momma. And we're going to be okay."

"What are you talking about?" Momma stares at me. I explain, but she just keeps asking me that same question over and over again. Eventually, it sinks in, and I get up and jump around the house shaking it so hard it feels like it's going to fall over. Momma's too weak to jump around, but she does nod along.

5

BRIELLE

Two Years Later

It has been two years since I got that check from the Wild Foundation and it has been one and a half years since Momma went into remission. Every three months she goes for a checkup, and the more checkups that come and go without a resurgence of cancer the better her luck is in surviving in the long run.

Every day, I am thankful for that check from that mysterious benefactor. I don't know why we were chosen, but I want more than anything to thank him or her in person. But even that won't do it justice. It's impossible to explain how I really feel about this. Because it's not just my Momma's life that that check saved. It also saved my life.

When Momma was dying, I was living my life day to day, week to week. I made no plans for the future. The future didn't really exist. I barely knew how I was going to get through the week. But now, the future is open and bright.

I even moved out!

I don't live too far now, only a few streets over, but Momma insisted on it.

"A young woman such as yourself needs her own space," she said. "What if you want to bring a guy over? Where are you guys going to hang out? In the living room, while I'm snoring in the back room?"

"Momma," I rolled my eyes. "I don't want to bring a guy over."

"Well, I want you too," she looked straight at me. "You're twenty-seven- years- old now. You've been taking care of me for almost seven years. That's a big burden. You should've been living your own life."

She's right, of course. But I can't say that. I don't regret a moment that I spent caring for her. But a small part of me does wonder how different my life could be.

"Besides," I remember Momma saying. "You need your own place so you can find a guy so you can finally give me grandchildren!"

Grandchildren! I've been caring for her for so long, I can't even imagine having the time in the day to care for children! Let alone a husband.

AND SO, with her insistence, I moved out. I got my own trailer a couple of streets away from hers. It's definitely nice to come home to my own place with everything put away neatly in its place. No boxes here. No clothes all over the floor. I have more time to focus on this now. And now, I even have time to focus on other things. Like my future.

My gaze goes to the course catalog laying on my brand-new kitchen table. Well, it's not brand-new, it's from the thrift store down the street, but it's nevertheless my kitchen table. All mine. I leaf through the course catalog. I wonder what else could be mine? Perhaps, I could have my own career. A nurse, maybe? I have a lot of experience now. The pay is really good, in comparison to a waitress, anyway. But I don't know if I can care for anyone anymore. Momma's cancer has really worn me out.

"Ding Dong! Ding Dong!" My new door bell goes off startling me. Who could that be?

"Yes, may I help you?" I open the door.

There's a mailman at the door. I've never seen him before, so he must be new.

"I've got a certified letter here for you, Miss," he says. He doesn't know my name.

"Where's Mr. Thompson, isn't he still working?"

He looks surprised that I know the other mailman's name.

"Yes, but he's transitioning to an internal role. So I'm going to be filling in for him sometimes."

I nod and sign for the letter.

THE ENVELOPE LOOKS FAMILIAR. The same fancy paper and the same elegant script which has saved Momma's life.

After he pulls away, I turn the envelope over. This time, it's not from the Wild Foundation. It's from someone named Mr. Francis Thompson. I open the envelope and take a deep breath. If they're asking for all the money back, I have no way of paying. We've spent it all!

Dear Ms. Brielle Elizabeth Cole,

WE HAVE RECENTLY LEARNED that your mother has made quite a recovery, and her cancer is now in remission. What great news!

We are pleased that you were able to put the money to such good use. And we are very happy for you.

However, we are now in need of your help. It is my pleasure to invite you to the Wild House for a brief residency, lasting no longer than a year. We hope you accept the invitation so that the process of you paying the debt back goes smoothly.

Sincerely,
Mr. Francis Whitewater

Certain words and phrases stand out. I read them over and over again, but they don't make any more sense.

Residency.

No longer than a year.

Debt.

What does that mean? What is he talking about? What debt?

"Well, you didn't think you got that money for nothing, did you?" Dottie asks when I show her the letter at work.

She's close to 90-years-old, and she's the only one who I trusted enough to tell her about the check. And I didn't even tell her anything until after half the money was spent and Momma was on her way to recovery.

"I don't know," I shake my head. "I guess I did."

Dottie laughs. "I've seen a lot in my long life, but this is a new one for me."

"What should I do?"

"I don't know what to do, child," she shakes her head. "But from the looks of this, the letter doesn't seem menacing at all. Maybe they just want you to work there until you pay off your debt."

"Work there? Where?"

"At the Wild House. Whatever the hell that is."

"But I didn't even know this was a debt. Don't they have the obligation to tell me? Shouldn't I sign for something if it was going to be a debt?"

"Perhaps, but I don't think this is any normal kind of debt. This isn't the bank. They would've never given you the money."

I know she's right, of course. No one gave us any money when we needed it. They all turned their backs on us.

"Well, do you think it's something sinister? Like some sort of brothel? Or prostitution ring?" I ask.

I don't know why my mind went there, except that I watch a lot of crime investigation shows on my days off.

Dottie thinks about it for a moment.

"I doubt it," she finally says.

"Those kinds of places usually promise you lots of money first and then use you up and toss you out. These people gave you a quarter of a million dollars first without even getting you to sign anything for it."

"And since I didn't sign anything for it, I technically don't have to do anything they say," I say. I feel my eyes lighting up with excitement.

"Well, technically, no," Dottie nods. "But I wouldn't want to play with Karma like that, honey. That might bring a whole lot of bad luck on you."

She's right, of course. I had to go. I owed a debt and if there was some reasonable and honest way that I could pay it back then I owed it to them to try.

6

BRIELLE

Two weeks later

WITHIN A WEEK of receiving the letter, I quit my job at the café. I had worked there for many years and I promised to come back, but I couldn't leave them hanging, I didn't know how long I would be away.

Before I quit my job, I called Wild House and spoke to Mr. Francis Whitewater, who came off quite polite and well spoken. He said that my duties at the Wild House would consist of acting as a personal assistant, answering emails and phone calls, and maybe participating in light cleaning and nursing. When I asked about the nursing aspect, he was very brief and practically refused to give out details, but said that someone had to be taken care of, but the nursing duties are mild. Nothing like the ones I had to perform for my mother.

After I had agreed to go on the phone, he sent me an email with the work contract, which I had to sign and return before I could go. I read through the contract carefully, and was surprised to learn that I was actually going to get paid for this job. Four times more money than I made at the café and I would also be provided with a one bedroom apartment in which to live on the property.

After all the details were ironed out, I finally told Momma what I was going to do. I didn't tell her about the initial letter, but I did say that I got a new job and it was more than five hours away from her, somewhere in central California. Without missing a beat, she wrapped her arms around me and gave me a warm and encouraging hug.

"I'm so so happy for you, Brielle," she whispered into my ear, her voice cracking. "I'm so happy that you're finally starting your life out. Going somewhere new. I will definitely come visit you soon!"

Come visit me? I had no idea if this was allowed or proper or acceptable. I didn't know anything about this place, but I agree.

"Yes, that will be great."

I still had a few months until then to figure things out.

To get to the Wild House, I had to take a plane to Chino, California and then a car. I was planning on driving, but Mr. Thompson insisted that I did not need a car there. I didn't believe him of course. There's no place in California that doesn't require a car, except maybe the city of San Francisco, but I eventually and reluctantly agreed. Momma and I had only one car and we share it. I can't take it away from her.

In the baggage claim area of the small local airport, I meet my driver. We drive for some time down a lonely two-lane road leading somewhere into the desert. Desert mountains rise on either side of us, far near the horizon. This isn't an unfamiliar sight. I'm used to the nature that far-flung places in the wilds of California have to offer.

During the drive, I try to talk to the driver, but he offers very little in way of information.

"I don't know, miss. You'll find out when you get there," he says over and over again. That's his canned response to almost every question I have about this whole experience.

We turn off the main highway and onto a lonely desert road. My heart starts to pound and matches the bumps in the road that we drive over. The car isn't your typical sedan. It's a tall Jeep, which is meant for off road. Just as I thought that the road couldn't be any more off road, we turn onto an actual off-road road. There are no signs, but the driver turns to the left at the sandy fork in the road. Now we're driving through the desert. Across its wide expanse and over little shrubs and around tall creosote bushes that dot the area.

Finally, somewhere in the distance, I see a large house. It's actually in the middle of nowhere. As we get closer, I make out the beautiful tall white columns that give it grandeur and stature. There are two large white lion statues at the gate. The driver pulls to the intercom and pushes the button.

"We're here," he says. The iron-wrought gates open and let us in. The Lions don't move but continue to stare somewhere into the distance, probably wondering the same thing that I am at this moment: how the hell did we get here.

The driveway is expansive and circular and the driver pulls up right to the steps of the mansion. I've never been to the White House, but this house looks just like it. The columns are a pristine ivory color. How the hell they keep them so white in the middle of this dusty desert is beyond me.

"Go on up," the driver says when he comes around and opens my door.

"What about you?" I ask. I don't know him, but I don't want him to leave. I have no idea what awaits me inside. I look at my phone and see that I don't even have one bar! There's absolutely no reception here.

"Oh, I'm not going in there, miss."

There? Why did he say it like that? My heart starts to pound harder. It's so loud, I can barely hear my own thoughts in my head.

The driver gets my two modest suitcases out of the trunk and takes them up the few steps to the porch. The porch is made of beautiful polished wooden slats and it seems to wrap all the way around the building.

There are two imposing double doors before me. The driver picks up the large metal door knocker and slams it into the door. After two knocks, the door finally opens.

"Ms. Brielle Cole," a small older gentleman says. He's dressed up like a butler from Downtown Abbey.

"My name is Mr. Francis Whitewater, it's my pleasure to meet you."

I shake his extended hand.

"May I help you with your bags?"

I nod, leave one bag on the porch and go inside with the other one.

"Let me show you to your room," he says walking past me.

When I enter the lobby, my mouth drops open. The ceilings are close to 20 feet high and gorgeous natural light permeates the space. The desert sun is rather harsh outside, but in here the temperature is a cool and comfortable 75 degrees, without a whiff of central air. There's a beautiful round marble entry table with a bouquet of flowers in the middle of the entry room the size of a ballroom and two winding staircases frame the table on either side, leading up to the second floor.

"What a beautiful…house?" I say. House doesn't seem like the right word. Mansion? Castle?

"Thank you. I'll let, Mr. Wild know that you approve."

"So, Mr. Wild? Is that who requested my presence here," I take the opportunity to ask.

"Yes, of course. I thought that was clear from the letter."

"No," I shake my head. "The letter wasn't very clear about much. The thing is, Mr. Whitewater, I don't even know who Mr. Wild is. I have no idea why he wants me here. Or what he expects me to do."

Mr. Whitewater turns to face me. "I'm not sure what you're trying to insinuate by that, Ms. Cole, but you are not expected to do anything that you are not 100% willing and interested in doing. Mr. Wild invited you here as a guest. There is nothing sinister about his intentions."

I nod politely. I'm trying to understand, but rich people have a way of saying things that don't make sense. Supposedly, I'm only here as a guest, but the letter was also quite clear about a certain debt that had to be paid. So what would happen if I didn't pay it?

Mr. Whitewater led me through the foyer, the gigantic living room with even taller windows, which looked out to the expanse of the desert in the background. The windows were so large, floor to ceiling, and clear that I felt like I was walking outside.

"You probably have some problems with birds here," I say. I don't know why I bring this up, but large floor to ceiling windows always make me wonder about birds.

"How do you mean?" Mr. Whitewater asks with a grave expression of concern on his face.

Now, I'm totally regretting bringing anything up at all. Me and my stupid mouth!

"Well, it's just that, the windows are so big and crystal clear…"

He stares at me, waiting to continue.

"I just think that you probably have a lot of birds flying into it."

Mr. Whitewater takes a moment to consider the situation. "You know, come to think of it, yes, we do. It's almost every morning or so that I find one or two dead birds laying on the back porch."

"Oh, how sad," I say. "Well, I guess that's something I can try to fix."

Mr. Whitewater smiles at me. "Perhaps, perhaps."

"You don't think so?" I ask. I'm usually quite good at reading people. Waitressing for seven years has taught me that if nothing else. But I find Mr. Whitewater difficult to read and analyze. Perhaps, it's his English accent that's throwing me off.

"No, not at all. I just wasn't sure that would be part of your job description."

"I'm not sure either. But I was told that I am here to be a personal assistant and caregiver of the place. Perhaps, within the scope of those duties, I can make some time to try to prevent the deaths of one or two birds per day."

I don't mean to be smug and condescending, but as soon as these words come out of my mouth, I realize that I am. Luckily, Mr. Whitewater lets it slide.

I follow him to the left wing of the house, past the kitchen the size of three doublewide trailers, without another word.

"Well, here we are," Mr. Whitewater reaches into his pocket and gets a keycard. He slides it into an opening on the card reader and then hands it to me.

"This is your room. And this is your card."

We walk into a spacious one-bedroom suite with a full entry way leading to the living room and a large bedroom. The living room and bedroom are separated by French doors and there's also another pair of French doors leading to the private patio outside of the bedroom.

"Wow, this is beautiful."

Mr. Whitewater puts down my bag.

"I'm glad that it's too your liking."

"Yes, definitely. Thank you."

Mr. Whitewater starts to leave but then turns around.

"Oh yes, I almost forgot. Mr. Wild is expecting you for dinner at 6 pm. There are dresses and shoes in the closet. And you are of course welcome to wear your own clothes as well."

I nod. But he doesn't let me off the hook that easily.

"Can I tell him that you are coming?"

"Yes, of course," I mumble.

Of course, I know that I'm supposed to meet this Mr. Wild at some point. I just didn't think it would be so soon. No, not so soon. It's not soon. It's in a few hours, and I thought I'd meet him right away. I just didn't think that it would be so formal. Dinner? Why doesn't he just come up here? Or I could come to his office? I don't know if I can manage a whole dinner.

After Mr. Whitewater excuses himself, I open the closet. The closet is almost as big as the bedroom!

I've seen these closets before. Walk-in closet with shelves lining all three walls and a large island in the middle. On elegant, real wooden hangers, I find five dresses. Pink, red, black, blue and green. Each one is more beautiful than the others. One is knee-length made of chiffon. One is short and tight with built in bra cups. I run my fingers over the dresses and inhale the luxury.

Below the dresses, I find 10 pairs of different kinds of shoes. All pristine, never worn, without one scuffed up bottom. The heels vary in size and I quickly try on each one. The flats are the most comfortable, but the high heeled five inch heels with red bottoms make me feel most like a woman.

"Oh my God! What am I doing here?" I say out loud walking out of the walk-in closet. "People don't do this for nothing. Why does he want me here? To live here?"

Crazy, anti-social thoughts flooded my mind. He wants something from me and whatever he wants isn't easy to get. But what? I shake my head. I don't know.

I sit on the couch and put my feet up on the soft upholstered coffee table. I need to decide what to do. Hours crawl by, but I am still at an impasse. Finally close to 5:45, I decide that I will go downstairs and find out what this is all about. I'm a guest here, at least so far, and I will act like a guest. But I won't do anything that I don't feel comfortable with.

I look at the dresses hanging in the closet. They are beautiful, of course. But I'm not a charity case. I don't know who this man is and I need to retain some power in this relationship. I open my suitcase and look for the best thing that I have. Jeans are too casual. Besides, I don't really have any without any holes in them. Tshirts are also too casual. Aha! A button-down shirt and a pair of khakis. Practical. Professional. Not too sexy. Not sexy at all, actually.

7

BRIELLE

I still had some time to kill before dinner. There was no television in the room. A part of me was relieved, yet another was horrified. My phone didn't work and, though I brought my laptop, there was also no internet connection to be found. What the hell did people do here? I wish that I brought some paperbacks from home. My mom has an extensive collection of romance books and a handful of those would at least keep me entertained in the evenings.

I walk over to the window. The sun is setting and hugging the whole world outside with a warm, comforting hue. This is the color of possibility. Nothing can go wrong in a world bathed in this color. I feel like that's true, but I'm afraid it's not. I look out of the window and see horses grazing in the distance. There's no grass to speak off, but hay is scattered for them on the ground and they stand with steadfast calmness, which puts me to ease.

I've never ridden a horse, but I've always wanted to. There were only a few girls from my high school who rode horses and both of their families were quite wealthy and owned many acres of ranch land. I always found the idea of living on a ranch very romantic, but now that I was on one, I wasn't so sure. The idea of Mr. Wild freaks me out. What kind of elusive and crazy millionaire would ask a stranger to come and live and work in his house for a year? What did he want me from me? My mind immediately went somewhere dark and scary and I wouldn't let it wander too much. Too much thinking, too many scary thoughts, are not good. Especially, since I have to be here for some time.

On the other hand, my mind continues wandering without my permission, this isn't mandatory. Of course, he could keep me here without my permission, but I have no indication that it's what he means to do. So far, everyone has been nothing but nice and professional. Maybe, there's nothing sinister about this place at all!

I LOOK at the clock again. I have ten minutes until dinner. Most girls would need more time, but I don't. I slowly change into my khakis and a pink button down shirt. Something about the pink shirt makes it clash with the khakis so I try on the blue polka dot button down shirt.

"Yes, this looks much better," I say out loud into the mirror. There's no one around. I'm not used to having so much privacy given that I grew up in a double-wide with my mom. And I'm kind of enjoying the space and the solitude.

"This looks great," I say to myself. I take out my hair tie and flip my head over. When I bring my head back up, my hair falls with much more volume than before. Though it's usually as straight as straw, today it's all in waves around my face.

"Not bad," I smile and run my fingers through it. "Not bad at all."

Makeup. The heat from the long ride from the airport has all, but melted off whatever little amount of eyeliner and mascara I'd applied earlier this morning.

I apply a generous amount of eyeliner with my mouth open. I'm not sure what opening my mouth does for eyeliner application, but it's been a habit since I was 13. I've also seen girls do it on television, so it must be how it's done.

When all of my makeup, hair and clothes were done, I again look in the mirror. And then at the clock. I still have 9 minutes left! How's that possible? Should I go down early? No, I decide. I can't go down early.

My eyes drift back to the closet. I open it again and look at the dresses. I run my fingers over the different fabrics. Each is different from the next. All are much more expensive than any fabric I've ever owned.

I start to unbutton my shirt and pulling off my pants before I even realize what I'm doing. Suddenly, I'm pulling on the dress with the thick taffeta skirt on the button. The dress poofs out at my hips and I love how small it makes my legs and waist look.

"Amazing."

I twirl and the dress continues without me. I try on the pair of high heels that are placed right underneath the dress. I've never heard of the company, but I love how pointy the front is and how high the heels are.

I twirl again in front of the window.

I feel like I'm a princess. The fabric feels amazing next to my skin. The taffeta skirt hides my hips and emphasizes my breasts. The polka dots make me feel young, friendly and alive.

I look back at the clock. I still have a few minutes before dinner. If I want to change.

"You should change," I say to myself in the mirror. But the girl who looks back at me doesn't want to.

"If I don't ever see Mr. Wild again, if I leave tonight after dinner, then at least I got to wear this beautiful dress once," I reason.

I'm rationalizing. Justifying. Trying to give myself reasons to wear it. But I don't need to. I want to wear it. That should be enough.

"Okay," I look in the mirror. "Okay, this is it."

I walk down the elaborate and ornate staircase in my taffeta polka dot dress and high heels. My steps are cautious and deliberate. All I hear is the sound my shoes make when they hit the marble and echo off the walls. The walls are lined with beautiful ornate rugs I've only seen in expensive stores on Rodeo Drive. The stairs are a little slippery and I hold on to the railing. Why they don't put some of those rugs on the staircase is beyond me.

I remember where the kitchen is and I see Mr. Whitewater in the distance. Near the dining room. I take a deep breath and nearly float the rest of the way over.

"Ms. Brielle Cole, thank you for coming," Mr. Whitewater says to me. He's holding a tray and one tall glass with something in it.

"Would you care for some champagne with strawberries?"

I nod and he hands me the glass.

"Mr. Wild is waiting for you in the library."

Library? I wasn't shown a library before! My heart skips a beat. I'm not sure who I'm more excited to see. Mr. Wild or the library. The presence of a library solves the entire problem of what the hell I'm going to do in my room when I'm not working.

Mr. Whitewater takes me down a hallway which was not part of today's tour. In the end, he turns off to the right into a large spacious room entirely covered in books. Books line every imaginable part of it, from floor to ceiling. The ceiling is about twenty feet, just like in the rest of the house. What really makes the place special is the large bay window overlooking an orange grove.

There's a man sitting there in the shadows. I can't see his face, but I can see his well fitted suit and handsome profile. His hair is brushed back and his nose reminds me a Roman emperor.

"Mr. Wild. May I present, Ms. Brielle Elizabeth Cole," Mr. Whitewater announces.

I've never been presented before! I don't know what to do. Mr. Wild gets up and approaches me. His walk is deliberate and considerate. His shoes are so shiny they are bouncing light into my eyes even though it's relatively dark in the library. So dark, in fact, that I can barely make out his face.

"Ms. Brielle Cole," Mr. Wild says. Immediately, his voice sounds incredibly familiar. But I can't place it. Do I know him? How in the world would I know him?

Finally, Mr. Wild steps into the light and I see his face.

It's him!

No, it can't be! Can it?

My mouth runs dry. I can't speak.

It's the guy from the café. The one who drives the Bentley. The one who asked me out twice!

"It's very nice of you to join me," Mr. Wild says extending his hand. I don't know what to do. I take his hand and bend down at the knees before him. Just a bit, but enough for him to notice.

"What are you doing?" Wyatt smiles. "Did you just curtsy?"

Wyatt tilts his head back and laughs. His laugh is deep and strong and the sounds of which echo around the books in the library.

"Don't laugh," I finally say. My mouth is still entirely dry, but I manage to get the words out without a crack.

"Why are you laughing?" I ask. I'm so embarrassed. I don't know what came over me. I didn't mean to curtsy. But I've never been presented before. For some reason, it seemed to be like the right thing to do. Agh, I'm so stupid! I feel my cheeks growing hot. But Wyatt doesn't stop laughing.

"Why are you laughing?" I ask again. Now, my embarrassment is turning into anger. I make a fist and I get ready to punch him. Maybe not in that beautiful face of his, but at least in the shoulder, or chest or stomach, at the very least.

"I'm sorry," Wyatt says, still chuckling. "I just never had anyone curtsy for me before. I gotta say, I kinda liked it. Maybe you can do it again later tonight."

"It was an accident. I'm definitely not going to do it again later tonight."

"Okay, okay. Sorry!" he says sarcastically. "I'm just having a good time with you Brielle. Lighten up."

I take a moment to collect my thoughts. The curtsy has definitely broken the ice, but it got us nowhere closer to where we needed to be. I have so many questions for this man. The last man on earth, I thought I would see.

"Why am I here, Wyatt?" I ask.

I'm trying to be as serious as I can be. Even though, a huge part of me is relieved that Mr. Wild is NOT some 70-year-old man with hemorrhoids.

"What do you mean?" he asks, nonchalantly. As if he has nothing to explain. Nothing to hide.

"Why am I here?" I shrug. "What do you want from me?"

He shifts his weight from one foot to another and looks down.

"I don't know. I don't really have an answer," he finally says.

"You don't? You brought me all the way over here and you don't have an answer?"

"No, not really," he shakes his head. "I just wanted you to come. You didn't want to go out with me..."

He doesn't finish his sentence. I wait for him to complete it.

"I didn't want to go out with you so you decided to bring me here for a year. Force me to work for you?"

That gets his attention. And insults him, judging from how red his face gets.

"You are free to leave anytime, Ms. Cole," Wyatt looks straight at me. "You're not my slave or anything like that. Who do you think I am?"

I shake my head. Now, it's my turn to get incensed. "No, I can't. Not really, though," I say.

"Yes, you can."

"You paid for my Momma's very expensive treatment, Wyatt. I really appreciate it. Why? Why did you do that?"

"Because I heard that she needed help. You needed help."

"But there are millions of people in the world to help. Why me?"

"Okay, there you got me," he shrugs. "I did it because I like you. I wanted to help you. I didn't want you to lose her. I heard she's doing really good."

"Yes, she is. And I'm very grateful for that. I want you to know that I am."

"Great, that's what I wanted to hear."

"But I still don't understand this," I wave my hands in between both of our chests. He grabs my hand and wraps his warm, strong fingers around each wrist. My heart skips a beat. I feel a surge of electricity pass through him to me. It's just a spark. But it makes me feel warm all over. All shivers and uncertainty that I'd felt before dissipates. Now, I just want him to kiss me. I want him to keep holding my wrists and for him to slam his body into mine.

"What are you doing?" I whisper. I don't know how long he's been holding my wrists, but I never want him to stop.

"I wanted you…" he whispers. Wyatt takes a beat and looks straight into my eyes. "I want you."

That's it. The words just hang there in between us. I don't want to breath in or out for fear that I will make them dissipate.

"You want me?" I whisper. He stares at me.

"You want me to do what?" I ask.

"Nothing," he shrugs. "Nothing you don't want to do. I just want you here."

I nod. I don't understand. But I don't really need to right now.

There's a knock at the door.

"Mr. Wild? Ms. Cole?" Mr. Whitewater says. "Dinner is ready."

Wyatt hands me my glass of champagne. At some point, I had put it down on the coffee table. But I have no memory of doing that.

"This is delicious," I whisper.

"Yes, it's quite lovely," Wyatt smiles. "We grow the strawberries ourselves. Fresh from the garden."

I bite into a strawberry. Its flavor explodes in my mouth and fills my nose and mouth of the most luxurious aroma I've ever experienced.

"Thank you for wearing one of the dresses," Wyatt whispers over my shoulder as I follow Mr. Whitewater down the hallway. "I know it wasn't easy for you."

I turn back. How does he know that? What the hell do you know about me? I want to ask. But I know he's right.

"I don't want to make you mad. I just want to say, thank you. You look stunning."

"You're welcome," I say. Though I have no idea why he's thanking me for it.

"It's just such a treat for me," Wyatt explains as if he knows what I was thinking.

His words send shivers up my spine.

The large 12-person table that I had seen in the dining room earlier that day is gone. Now, there's a small table there instead. It's elegantly appointed with sparkling silverware and crystal glasses. The plates are ivory white and the pottery is so magnificent I can't help but touch it.

"I love these plates," I say running my fingers over the middle of my plate. Then I realize that this is probably really not polite.

"I'm sorry, I shouldn't have done that," I say, embarrassed.

"No, it's okay," Wyatt laughs. "I didn't know someone could love plates."

I stare at him as if he was speaking a foreign language. "What are you talking about? These are magnificent! Look at how many little man-made imperfections there are in the middle. These are not factory made. They are crafted by an artisan. A very special artist."

He smiles at me. "You know, you're quite a surprise Brielle."

8

WYATT

She sits across from me staring at my mother's Mexican plates. She is doe-eyed and I want nothing more than to grab her and kiss her. Her innocence is enchanting and contagious. She's making me look at the plates my mother has bragged about for ages in a completely new way.

"You know, these plates are from Mexico," I say. "My mother brought them back with her many years ago. Apparently, they are quite unique and expensive because they are so plain. Mexican pottery isn't known for that."

Brielle's eyes open even wider than before. Now, I have her full attention. I just wish we weren't talking about fuckin' plates.

"Oh wow," she says running her fingers lightly against the grain of her plate. I want more than anything to be that plate. No, I want my cock to be that plate. I want her to run her fingers so carefully and lovingly along the curve of my erect cock.

"Wyatt?"

"Huh?" I come back to reality. Unfortunately.

"I just asked if you know what time period these are from."

"Oh, before the revolution. Mexican revolution. So at least at the beginning of last century."

When can we stop talking about the goddamn plates?

Finally, Mr. Whitewater emerges with two servants. They are carrying two plates.

"Pine nuts and kale salad with strawberries," Mr. Whitewater presents the food.

Brielle smiles and the world lights up.

"This looks delicious," she whispers and smiles at me and then back at Mr. Whitewater.

I pick up my glass to make a toast, but she has already dug into her salad.

"Oh, I'm so sorry," she swallows quickly and drops her fork. Her crudeness makes me horny.

"No, it's okay. I just wanted to say thank you for joining me here. It's a pleasure."

I have a whole speech planned out, but I leave it at that. She waits for me to continue, but I don't. Something is making me tongue- tied. And I'm never tongue-tied.

"Thank you," she smiles. We clink glasses.

The rest of dinner goes without a hitch. We don't speak much and when we do we are consumed with formalities. By the time, the dessert comes, I realize that this wasn't the best idea. I shouldn't have made this dinner so formal. She feels awkward and her awkwardness is making me feel uncomfortable. This place, this formality, isn't her. It's not me either. I just thought that it would be impressive. It worked on so many other girls that I'm lost as to what I should've done.

After dinner, I walk her back to her room. She walks a few steps ahead of me and I watch the way the taffeta under the dress bounces as she walks. I want to push it up and wrap my fingers around her ass.

"Did you have a good time?" I ask when we reach her door.

"Yes, very much so," Brielle smiles at me. "Dinner was delicious."

"And besides dinner?"

"You mean with you?"

I nod.

"Yes, I had a good time. To tell you the truth, I'm really glad you didn't end up being some 70-year-old creep. I had no idea who Mr. Wild was when I got here."

"Well, I'm not 70-years-old. Whether or not, I'm a creep is for you to decide."

I take a step forward, and she takes a step back. Suddenly, there's nowhere to go. Her head hits the back of the wall. I take another step forward.

I take her chin and tilt her head toward mine. Our lips touch, and I run my tongue on the side of her lips. She tastes like honey and lavender. She smells like the cheesecake, which we just ate for dinner. I pull her face closer to mine, and she wraps her hands around my shoulders. My cock grows large and pushes into her taffeta. She steps up on her tip toes, and my cock slides just a bit in between her legs.

Our kisses grow stronger and more powerful. I am thrust into a passion the kind of which I had never felt before. I grab her breasts and pull on the straps of her dress.

"Wyatt," Brielle whispers.

"Brielle," I manage to say. I kiss her neck. The urgency in my kisses intensifies, and I run my fingers up her naked leg.

"Wyatt," she pushes on me. I push back on her and continue to kiss her.

"Wyatt, stop!" her voice is powerful and needy. But I continue to kiss her. She's feeling just like I am. She must be!

"No, no, no, I can't," I whisper.

"Wyatt, stop!" she knees me in the balls. Shooting pain surges through my body and I drop to the floor.

"What the hell, Wyatt?"

"I'm sorry…" I whisper. I can't say it any louder. I'm laying on my back in the fetal position on the floor. I hear Brielle go into her room and lock the door. After a few minutes, the pain subsides. And I manage to scramble up to my feet.

I knock on her door. No one answers. I knock again, and for some reason try the door knob.

"It's locked, you asshole!" Brielle says.

"I'm sorry. I'm really really sorry, Brielle."

"Go away!"

"Please, Brielle. I'm really sorry. You don't have to let me in…"

"I know that! I mean, what did you think? You invite me here, get me a pretty dress, wine and dine me, and I'll just do whatever you want? I'm not a whore, Wyatt."

"I know," I say. "I never meant for it look like that. I just got carried away. I thought we were both feeling something, Brielle. I didn't mean to take it too far."

"Well, you did. And you're an asshole. When a girl says no, it means no. Keep that in mind for the future."

I'm so embarrassed. I can't believe this happened. I can't believe I did that.

"I honestly thought that we were both into it, Brielle. Please. You've got to believe me." My voice cracks a bit at the end.

"Fuck you!" Brielle says. "Oh yeah, and I'm leaving tomorrow morning."

She can't! I will stop her! She has no right! "You are?" I ask. Please, don't.

"I've decided that I'm not in debt to you," she says. "You paid for my Momma's treatment knowing that full well. And I'm not going to sleep with you. Not for any amount of money. Not even for a quarter of a million dollars."

She's right, of course. I did all that knowing that. I just thought that maybe as a thank you. No, that's not right. I wanted her to want me. I didn't want her to just sleep with me once. There's something about her that makes me want more. It's like she has some sort of spell on me.

"Okay," I finally say. "I understand. I'm leaving now."

I walk back to the library. I don't know where I'm headed. I'm just lost. Distraught. Ashamed. Who was that person back there? Not me, for sure. Brielle's right. I was an asshole. Am an asshole. She deserves much better than that. Who knows how far I would've taken it if she hadn't kneed me in the balls.

"Agh, I'm such an idiot!" I say out loud. The words echo across the library chamber.

I hit my fist on the built-in bookshelves.

"Dammit!" I say. Now, my hand is hurting, and my heart is pounding even faster than before. I take a deep breath and look up.

The bookshelves are stacked three high with old books, but only one stands out. Charlotte Bronte's Jane Eyer. The library is poorly lit, but this book seems to have a spotlight on it. I look out of the window and see the bright yellow moon looming high in the sky.

She'll like this, I decide. I pick up the first edition and flip through the pages. She won't be able to throw this gift away, I decide.

There's my grandfather's old writing desk in the corner. I sit down and open the top. I take a small piece of decorative paper from the top shelf and pick up the old ink pen, which miraculously still writes.

BRIELLE,
This is a first edition of Jane Eyer. I hope you like it. I hope you accept this gift as my apology. I'm sorry.
Love,
Wyatt

I READ THE NOTE OVER. Of course, she will know it's a first edition. It says so in the front! I ball up the piece of paper and toss it in the trash can.

BRIELLE,
I'm sorry. I didn't mean to do any of that this evening. Well, that's not true. I did mean to kiss you. I loved kissing you. I loved tasting you on my lips — I want to taste your sweet cunt.

I READ this note over again and again then crumple it up. This is supposed to be an apology. And like all apologies, it will have to be partly true and partly untrue. I can't say everything I want to say. Otherwise, she won't accept it.

I WRITE ANOTHER NOTE. My final note. When I'm finished, I wait for the ink to dry before carefully folding it and place it in front of the title page. In the back of the writing desk, I find a small box, which ends up being the perfect fit for the book. Now it really looks like a gift.

I WALK BACK to Brielle's room and knock on the door. She doesn't answer. I don't know if she can hear me, but I decide to leave the box right outside. After trying one last time, I finally give up and walk away.

I've done all I could. At this point, I have no choice but to accept her decision. Whatever it might be. No matter how much I hate it.

9

BRIELLE

I spent the night crying into my pillow. How dare he do that to me? I sob. My pillow is damp from all the tears I shed. I'm not just crying over what happened. I'm crying over what it means. He was such an asshole and now I can never trust him again. I had to physically push him off me. Who the hell does that? How far would he have gone if I wasn't strong to push him away? To knee him in his balls?

Millions of thoughts swirl in my head. I hate him. And I love him. I want to kiss him. And I want to punch him. I want him to knock harder on my door and knock it down. And I want him to go away and leave me alone. My makeup is running down my face and my eyes burn from all the cheap mascara getting into them. Finally, when they start to burn so much that it becomes unbearable, I force myself to go to the bathroom and wash my face.

"Why do you have to be such an asshole?" I say to myself in the mirror as if I'm talking to Wyatt. "We had such a great dinner. You were lovely. Polite. I was kind of a mess, but you weren't. You were…a gentleman. And then that. That happened. How can I forgive that?"

I shake my head. No, I can't forgive that. Because next time it might be much worse. I sigh.

I tried. I really tried. I came here. I had dinner. I even kissed him. This is all that he could've expected from me. It's okay if I go now. I've tried to repay my debt. It didn't work out. Because of *him*. So it's not my fault, right? Right.

There's a knock at the door. Then another. And another. I don't answer. I've said enough. I don't want to argue anymore. My mind is made up. In the morning, Mr. Whitewater is ordering me a cab or a driver and I'm getting out of here.

The following morning, I sleep in late. I'm still in bed at eight am. The bed is made of feathers and softness beyond my imagination. I feel like I've slept on a cloud and I'm not looking forward to going home to my thin, uncomfortable mattress at home. I got for $99 on sale, and it feels like it.

I pull on the most comfortable pair of jeans I own and my favorite turquoise tank top. Someone once told me that I looked great in turquoise, and I've stocked my closet with turquoise tops ever since. I always thought they were right, but this morning, I'm not so sure. I look pale and tired. A big part of me is regretting the fact that I'm leaving. But I'm not sure I have the courage to go back on my word.

There's a light knock on the door.

"Who is it?"

"Good morning, Ms. Cole," Mr. Whitewater says after I open the door.

"Good morning, Mr. Whitewater," I say with a yawn.

He looks like he has been awake for hours. His hair is perfectly groomed and coiffed, and his suit is starched and ironed, or whatever one does to suits to keep them wrinkle-free.

"Mr. Wild told me that you will be leaving this morning. I'm sorry to hear that."

"Yes, me too," I nod. I am sorry. I wish this weren't happening.

He doesn't say another word, doesn't make a move either. I stare at him. What's wrong? Slowly, his eyes tilt down. I follow them to the floor and see a light pink box.

"Oh, what's this?" I ask.

"I'm not sure. But it's for you," Mr. Whitewater says. He quickly takes a step back and turns away from me to give me some privacy.

I EXAMINE the box carefully in my hand. The cardboard looks old and smells a bit like cake. I carefully open the flap and peek in. It's a book! A book?

I pull out the book and let the box drop to the ground. Oh, my God. My heart starts to pound. Is this really what I think it is?

A first edition of Jane Eyer!?!?

The book is rather small and weathered, but otherwise it's in excellent condition. I flip through the pages. The pages are thicker near the front. Carefully, I flip the pages one at a time until I get to the title page and discover a note. It's written on perfumed paper, the kind that you see in expensive paper stores. There's a delicate floral design gracing each of the ends.

I open the note.

It's from Wyatt. I see his name written in beautiful, careful script on the bottom. The W is elongated and flowery, the y is elegant and the two sets of t's are defiant and proud.

Dear Brielle,

I'm sorry. For everything.

You deserve a lot better than me, of course. But please give me another chance.

Yours,

Wyatt

Yours. I like the sound of that. I've never had anyone who was mine, in that way. My heart skips a beat again. And then another.

Mr. Whitewater clears his throat and I remember that he's still here.

"I think I need a moment, Mr. Whitewater," I finally manage to utter. I go back into my room and close the door.

"Oh my God," I whisper. "A first edition of Jane Eyer!"

I press the hardback book to my breasts and inhale its beautiful musty smell. This book has been around for hundreds of years and now it's mine. It belongs to me.

But can I accept it if I decide not to stay here? I want to. He owes me an apology and this was a marvelous apology.

My thoughts drift back to Wyatt. Suddenly, I remember the softness of his lips. And how they danced with mine to a tune that only we heard. I remember how hot I felt in between my legs and how much I wanted him to push up my taffeta skirt and let me wrap my legs around his strong, powerful torso.

He wasn't alone in feeling what he was feeling. I was there right along with him. We shared a chemical and electric connection. I was drawn to him as if he were a magnet and I had trouble pulling away as well. I loved how hard his cock felt pushing into me, pressing me to the wall. I wanted to rip off his clothes. I wanted him to rip off mine. And then it was just too much. In a split second, it was suddenly too much.

I don't know what I should do. I want to stay, but I also want to go. I want to stay to get to know Wyatt more. And I want to run away from this place and it's games.

The sound of a startled horse scares me and I walk over to the window. I lift the window and open the shutters. I didn't notice it last night, but there are stables to the right of me. The horse makes another piercing cry sending shivers over my body.

"It's okay, Sebastian. It's okay, guy," Wyatt says. I can't see him, but his voice is firm and commanding and I really believe that it's going to be okay.

Suddenly, they emerge. Wyatt is dressed in jeans, a pair of brown boots, and a simple white t-shirt. He's tan and his sweaty body glistens in the sun. His hair looks wet, either from sweat or water. He's riding a tall black horse with a thick black mane that flies up with each gallop. They are moving as one. I look closer, and I see that the horse is not wearing a saddle. Wyatt is riding bareback!

The horse and the rider dance together for a few moments in a circle. The horse kicks up swirls of dust, which in the sunlight look like periwinkle. And then suddenly, the horse shifts his weight and raises his front legs in the air.

"Oh wow," I whisper in awe. Wyatt remains in place on his back holding on by nothing but his powerful thighs. It looks like the horse is going to land on his front legs and then morph into a trot, but he doesn't. Instead, he lands hard on his front hooves and lifts his back hooves up high in the air. And then he does it all again.

My smile fades quickly after I realize that something's going wrong.

"Oh my God," I whisper and bring my hands to my face. "No, no, no…"

But it's too late. The horse bucks one last time, and this time, Wyatt doesn't hold on. I see him flying through the air. He misses the chain-link fence by less than a foot and lands flat on his back.

"Oh my God!" I scream. My voice echoes around the room, but Wyatt doesn't get up.

"Get up! Please get up," I scream, but he doesn't.

For a brief second, I consider running to the back of the room, down the long hallway, down the winding staircase, out of the front door, and around the entire 10,000 square foot house. But then I see a simpler way down.

"What are you doing?" Mr. Whitewater enters my room.

I'm already hanging out of the window, half of my body is on the roof of the patio.

"Wyatt is hurt, call 911!"

I climb down the post of the patio, jump into the orange grove below and run toward Wyatt.

I finally reach him. His face is so pale that it's the color of those white Mexican plates from dinner. All blood has drained from his face, and his lips are blue.

"Wyatt? Wyatt?" I scream. I want to shake him and bring him back to life. But I'm afraid he has broken something in his body, and that will make it worse.

"Wyatt? Wyatt? Please wake up. Please, please, please," I shout cradling my arms around him.

Mr. Whitewater runs over.

"How is he? Oh my God. He's unconscious."

I nod. I don't know what else to do.

"I just called 911, but they won't be here for some time."

"What, why?" I demand to know.

"Twenty minutes at the earliest," he says and puts the receiver back to his ear. "They say that we shouldn't move him until they get here. He might've broken his back."

The world fades to black with those words. 'He might've broken his back' is all I hear in my head over and over again. The paramedics arrive sometime later. They have to scream at me to get out of the way. I don't move. I don't even know if I can move. Someone pushes me out of the way and they take Wyatt away. They strap him onto a gurney and roll him to the ambulance.

I can't go along. No one can. They tell me and Mr. Whitewater that we can follow along behind the ambulance if we want.

I'm in a daze. I don't know what to do. I follow Mr. Whitewater to his car.

"Are you sure you want to come? I thought you wanted to leave this morning? You still can, if you want to."

I stare at him. All thoughts of leaving have all but dissipated. I don't even know what he's talking about. All I know is that I can't leave now. I don't know what's wrong with him and I can't leave until I find out. What if he needs my help?

Twelve hours later.

I've spent the last twelve hours in the hospital looking at magazines and mindlessly reading books that I did not understand on my phone. I read the words, but they don't make any sense. I don't know who wrote them or for what reason. The only thing that makes sense to me is the pictures. I leaf through the celebrity magazines and pay close attention to which movie stars have lost and gained weight. Which ones were pregnant. Which ones got engaged and which ones got divorced. It's all things that I used to find interesting, but now none of it makes any sense.

This hospital reminds me of the one back home, where I waited for hours for my mom to get out of her various surgeries. Time stands still here. It's as if the waiting room is some secret time travel chamber in which I can go into and not age for hours and days and months. I age, of course. I noticed it whenever I went into the bathroom and looked at the horror that was my face, but I never felt time passing. Not even one second.

Breathe, I say to myself. Breathe.

I take a deep breath. And then another. And another. I feel a little better, but as soon as I look around, all of my thoughts and concerns and regrets creep back in.

A doctor who is in charge of Wyatt and his condition comes out from behind the double doors with a smile on his face.

"Wyatt's awake now," he tells Mr. Whitewater. "He's one lucky young man. Even though both of his legs are broken."

Broken legs. I sigh. He is lucky.

"Wait here," Mr. Whitewater tells me. I have no right to go see Wyatt. I'm not really anybody to him. Barely an employee. Still, I hope that I can go in to see him.

"And he doesn't have any brain damage?" Mr. Whitewater asks the doctor.

"No, not that I can tell. But it's too soon to know for sure."

I wait for what seems like a century for Mr. Whitewater to come back. Now time is positively moving backward. I wonder if it's now 1993. Finally, he comes out.

"He'd like to see you," Mr. Whitewater says.

"How is he?"

"Fine. Definitely all there."

I SMILE. A wave of relief sweeps over me.

10

WYATT

Brielle walks into my hospital room carefully and cautiously. It's as if she's walking on eggshells.

"It's okay," I say. "Don't be afraid." I sit up in my bed, trying not to look so sickly and powerless even though I have a pounding headache.

"How are you?" she asks sheepishly.

Her hair falls into her face slightly as she walks and she pushes it aside without much regard. Her lips look soft and exquisite even under the harsh fluorescent lights of the hospital room. Her skin is tan and her cheeks are full of color. Brielle is wearing a long sleeve hoodie and she wraps her arms around her shoulders as if she is trying to hold on to the entire world.

"I'm good. Fine," I say confidently. It's almost true. I want it to be true. I'll act like it is until it became true.

"Broke both legs," I say nudging at the cast. "Imagine the luck."

"It could've been much worse, Wyatt," she comes closer. I love the sound of my name in her mouth.

"Nah," I wave my hand. But she slaps it away.

"No, I'm serious. It could've been much much worse. I saw you out there. You passed out. You were unconscious. I thought you would go into a coma and never wake up."

"Hah, like you'd care. You'd just be happy that you got off the hook," I joke.

She stares at me and raises her hand to slap me again. This time across the face. But something stops her.

"Fuck you, Wyatt. Fuck you for even thinking something that terrible."

That was a pretty shitty thing to say. I shake my head. "I'm sorry. I didn't mean that. I was just trying to make you laugh."

"How would that make me laugh, exactly?"

"I don't know. I'd shrug, but my shoulders hurt too much."

This one does make her laugh. She opens her lips just a bit and lets out a small, willowy laugh. The world is alright again.

"How did this happen?" Brielle asks after a few silent moments.

"That's what you get for riding a four-year-old stallion bareback," I laugh.

Her face turns white. "What do you mean? Are you joking again?"

I shake my head no. And then suddenly, something comes over me. And I tell her something I never would otherwise.

"I was really upset that you were leaving. That I did that to you. Disrespected you like that. But I want you to know that it was really an accident. I must've not heard you or something. I would never keep going beyond what you said was okay. I'm not that guy."

I stop and look at her. She waits for me to continue.

"So I was really angry with myself over the whole thing. Over what I did. Over the fact that you were now scared of me. And leaving. That's the last thing I wanted. So this morning, I went for a walk and ended up in the stables. I saw Sebastian. He's a powerful thoroughbred. But he's not broken yet. He's wild and crazy, and I felt wild and crazy at that moment. It was like we were breathing the same air and feeling the same energy. I opened the gate and he let me get on top of him. I really thought we were connecting, and we wanted the same thing. But I was just feeling crazy. He ignited something within me, some long forgotten feeling of hope and love and wildness. And so I urged him outside of the stable. And that's when it got bad. He started to buck, and he wouldn't slow down long enough for me to get off. And then I just flew off."

"You remember it all?"

"I remember every single moment."

"And what about afterward?"

"No," I shake my head. "Once I hit the ground, I don't remember anything."

She looks at me. Tears well up inside of her eyes. One large tear breaks free and rolls down her cheek. I reach out and wipe it off her face.

"I was so scared, Wyatt. You were just laying there. Motionless. Unconscious. I wanted to shake you so much, but I was afraid something was broken. And then..."

Her voice drops off and she looks out of the window. A tiny sparrow dances on a branch. We both watch the sparrow for a moment before she turns back to me.

"And then?" I ask.

"And then I thought that maybe it was even worse than that. You didn't wake up Wyatt. Not for a long time."

I nod.

"You scare me, Brielle," I finally say.

"What do you mean?"

"I don't know exactly. But I feel something for you and it scares me."

"Don't be silly," she waves her hand and smiles. "How can I scare you?"

I try to shrug again. Again I feel pain.

"Come here," I say and wave my index finger to get her to come closer to me.

"What?" she leans down.

"You scare me," I whisper and press my lips up to hers. I lift my body a bit toward hers and my neck throbs in pain.

I sigh in pain when I pull away.

"Are you okay?" she says with a smile licking her lips.

"No," I shake my head. "But it was worth it."

THAT EVENING, the nurse gives me some morphine, and I fall asleep quickly. When I wake up in the morning, my back is throbbing, and I find Brielle half asleep in the chair.

"Hey, you're awake," she smiles at me.

"What are you doing here?" I ask. "I can't believe you slept the whole night here."

"Oh, I just dozed off. It's no big deal."

"No, it is," I say. "Thank you."

"I'm going to get us some coffee," she jumps up to her feet.

I'm jealous of the spring in her step and I wish more than anything that I could jump as well. I've only been in bed for one day and the thought of not being active for another two months scares me to death.

"Brielle…"

She turns at the door. Her hair leaps one last time before landing softly around her shoulders.

"Yes?"

"I was just wondering…" I don't know how to phrase the question exactly. She waits for me as I try.

"I was just wondering if you were planning on going back home today?"

"No," she shakes her head. A wave of relief sweeps over me, but I'm not sure if I have been clear enough.

"And tomorrow?" I ask.

Suddenly, it hits her what I'm asking. She walks back to my bed.

"I'm not going home for awhile Wyatt. But under one condition."

"What's that?"

"If you promise me that we will be friends. Just friends."

I thought about that for a moment. Just friends was better than nothing. "Okay," I nodded.

11

WYATT

How do you know if you truly love someone?

There was a time in my life when I never believed in love. I grew up in a world of privilege. My two brothers, Gatsby, and Atticus, and my sister, Ophelia, were raised by our nannies and had everything we ever wanted. Our parents had houses in Los Angeles, New York, Montana. An apartment in Paris. And another one is being built in Dubai.

When we were little, the family had more cars than I can even count – our father, Dr. Wild – is an avid collector. We each got a new car of our choosing as soon as we turned 16 and each one of us promptly crashed it soon after. I think it was O, we've always called Ophelia, O, who kept her first car, a brand new Mercedes, the most expensive class of that year, the longest. Six months, I believe.

My mother never cooked, but every night that we had dinner at home, we always had a delicious gourmet meal prepared by our personal chef. Our birthdays were lavish and expensive. Each one probably cost as much as a regular couple's wedding. They were extravagant with different themes and costumes and close to 400 guests each time. That doesn't sound like a fun birthday party for a five-year-old, but the entire school was invited so most of them were.

Our exclusive private school didn't have a school bus to get us to school, and the responsibility fell to our nannies to deliver us there and pick us up after each of our after school activities. O did theater. Gatsby and I played lacrosse. Atticus was in the band.

Our parents were always there to cheer for us – always physically present – and yet emotionally and metaphysically away. It's hard to explain now, difficult to put into words, but it was as if they were never really there.

Ever since I can remember, our parents had their own lives. My father, the renowned doctor and later the founder of a prosperous pharmaceutical company, worked late into the night and all weekends. He was always traveling and running meetings.

My mother had her philanthropic activities. She was the head of a number of boards that raised money for a variety of noble causes. She didn't get paid, but she worked nearly as hard as he did. And organized all of our days and the house staff on top of all that.

It's maybe cruel to say this, but my parents gave me the impression that love only meant one thing. My parents said that they loved us, but their love was complicated. It came with expectations and, inevitable, disappointments. It was never the kind of love often featured in movies. They were never mushy and hopeful and exuberant. They were both too busy with either work or their social obligations to really show love. Or at least, the way I expected it to be.

And so, coming back to my original thought. How do you know if you truly love someone? How am I expected to know if I love someone if their love was the kind of love I had only ever known?

Before I broke both of my legs riding a wild stallion, I never had time to think about these things. But now that I've been bed bound for more than six weeks, it seems all I do is think. I had to remain active somehow and my mind was the only place I had left.

Brielle enters the room carrying two cups of tea on a tray. She has been here for six weeks. Six of the happiest weeks of my life. I have never been immobile for this long before and yet her presence has made it, somehow, bearable. If it weren't for her, I'd be tearing my hair out. I'd be drunk all day just to pass the time. And yet, with her here, we find things to do that do not involve going outside much or using our legs.

I THINK I'm falling in love with Brielle. Her long hair, her tender eyes, her soft skin. I don't know anything about love, I'm the first the admit it. Yet, I also know that I've never felt this way about anyone before. Sometimes, when I see her, my heart jumps into my throat and I forget to breathe.

Other times, when she's away from me for a couple of hours, I feel anxious and uncertain. I don't know what to do with myself and spend the hours just looking out of the window or staring aimlessly at the television screen. I can't read a word that makes sense. All I can do is wait for her to return.

Brielle has been bringing me breakfast, lunch, and dinner and has made Mr. Whitewater all but useless. The responsibility of those things would've fallen to him. But she asked him if she could do it. I think she likes being useful. In fact, I've never met someone who enjoys being useful so much. It's almost as if she really loves taking care of me.

I feel myself falling in love with Brielle, even though I'm not sure if I know what that means. But does anyone? Isn't love just some sort of feeling that bubbles up from within us, from some place deep within our core that we didn't even know existed.

There is one problem, however. And it's a big one. We – Brielle and I – have decided to keep things professional. I believe that the only reason she's even here is that our relationship is now strictly professional. Or so she has called it that once. But in reality, it's not professional at all. Only a fool would think that our interaction is professional. We are more like friends. Close, close friends. And it's clear, at least I think it is, that I want more.

"What a beautiful morning, right?" she says plopping down on the couch next to me. "What do you want to do today?"

I want to kiss you and undress and lay in bed looking at and exploring your naked body until dinner. I want to say this to her, but instead I lie.

"Not sure, whatever," I shrug and remember her hurtful words.

"No more kissing, no more romance, or whatever it was that was happening between us," she said in my hospital room. I felt woozy from all the pain killers, but I remember each one of her words as if she said it a minute ago. "I just want to work here for the year, like I'd agreed, and be friends."

"Okay," I had agreed.

"You promise?" she asked.

"This is one of my conditions of staying. The only one."

I remember looking into her deep brown eyes and nodding. Then agreeing verbally to the only thing that would keep her in my life.

"You feeling alright?" she asks. Neither of us has said a word in a few moments. She touches my hand with hers sending shivers up and down my legs, as always. My cock grows hard and I press down on it trying to calm it. Ever since we'd decided to be friends, she started touching me more and more. More than she ever had before. But the touching is not sexual, at least not on her part. Just a pat of the hand, a small hug, a nudge. But each touch still makes me get hard.

I want her. I want her up against the wall. On the bed. Outside in the desert. In the shower.

"Hey, Wyatt?" she asks leaning close to me with a look of concern on her face. "How are you, today? Is everything okay?"

"I'm good," I fake a smile. "Why?"

"Something seems off," she shrugs. "Oh, I almost forgot, I got your pills, here."

I stare at her. Brielle mentions the pills in the same nonchalant way she has for the last six weeks. But this is the first day that I turn them down.

"Nah, I'm feeling okay. I don't think I need them today."

Her face lights up. "That's great!" she wraps her arms around me. "I'm so happy. You're making so much progress. Maybe you'll be able to take the casts off soon, too."

Now, there's a thought. To stand up and hold my body weight with my own two feet. I've taken that for granted for so many years. And then when I suddenly couldn't stand up on my feet and had to use crutches…the helplessness that came with that was unimaginable.

I smile with my whole body at the thought of taking the casts off.

"Yeah, I can't wait," I say. "I hate being a blimp. I feel like I'm totally useless. And like I'm getting fat."

Brielle laughs. A small quiet laugh that only gives me a small peek at her perfect white teeth. Then she looks me up and down.

"No, not at all."

"You have no idea how hard this has been for me. I mean, I know it hasn't been easy for you at all, waiting on me all the time. Which again, you don't really have to do. We have staff here for that," I say.

She starts to say something, but I cut her off. I know what she's going to say. She is the staff, she's happy to do it, or something in that vein.

"That's not what I want to say. What I mean is that it's been really hard for me to be so inactive for so long. I love being outdoors. I love riding horses. Playing basketball. Football. Baseball. Whatever. Using my body is a huge part of my life. And these past six weeks, it's like I've become someone else. I couldn't do that. And if it weren't for you...I would've been completely lost. It would've been much harder. So what I'm really trying to say, very artfully, is thank you. Thank you so much for being here. And being you."

Brielle takes a moment to internalize what I've said. Then she leans close to me. It takes all of my strength not to place my lips on hers. But I've long made myself a promise that it would be her, this time, who has to make the first move.

"It has been my pleasure," she whispers in my ear and pulls away.

Brielle jumps off the couch and the mood in the room changes. I watch her walk over to the large floor to ceiling window looking out onto the desert in front of us. A large raven perches on top of a crooked Joshua tree in the distance and then flies away.

"I finally found some tape and I'm going to take care of that bird problem," she says. By bird problem, she means that too many birds are flying into our spotless window and killing themselves. Mr. Whitewater, who washes that window almost every other day, isn't going to be happy. And we both know it.

"You know, he has been hiding this thing from me for all of these weeks," she says with a smile and picks up the roll of duct tape from the tray. "I've been asking him for it forever."

"What can I say, he loves keeping that window clean."

"I know he does, and the view from it is beautiful. But we can't just sit by and do nothing as birds continue to kill themselves on it practically every day."

"I guess not," I chuckle.

"Where do you think I should put it?" Brielle asks.

Over my hands and then to the headboard so that I can't touch you as you go down on me. And then I will wrap it around your hands and do the same to you.

Of course, I don't say any of that out loud. Instead, I point to a few spots on the window, which have resulted in the largest amount of casualties.

"You know, I talked to my mother again this morning," Brielle says as she tapes the window.

"Oh yeah, how is she?" I ask. I only mildly care. Don't get me wrong, I'm glad she's doing better but mainly because that means that Brielle doesn't have to go back home and take care of her.

"She's doing even better than before," she smiles.

The $250,000 check that I sent her for her mother's treatment was worth that smile alone. Brielle starts telling me all the details about how her mother's feeling. Her breathing is improving, not much pain in her hips, blah, blah, blah. All the information comes into one ear and goes out the other. I'm not paying attention. Not even a little bit.

Instead, my mind drifts elsewhere. I look at Brielle's round butt and the way it fills out her jeans. Her jeans have little decorative hearts on the back pockets and they draw my eye on the roundest part of her body. I don't know why clothing designers put them there. Do they know that they make women's butts look irresistible? Is that the whole point? Do the women know just how hard it is to look away from those two little hearts? Does Brielle?

When she turns to face me and tell me something else about her mom's condition, my gaze runs up her body. Brielle's small waist accentuates her hips, making them appear wider than they really are. And then suddenly, I land on her breasts. She doesn't wear a bra often, but her breasts are firm and erect. When the temperature in the room falls below 75 degrees Fahrenheit, her nipples get erect and resemble the tips of a ripe strawberry. I've gotten into the habit of turning down the furnace and praying each morning that today would be the day that she again chooses to go without a bra.

"Hey, are you listening?" Brielle asks.

"Yeah, so your mom is happy with the new doctor?" I parrot the last thing that she said back to me. I developed this talent of reiterating the last line that someone said back in sixth grade and it served me well way after I was done with formal education.

My words put her at ease and she continues on with her story while I curse myself for ever agreeing to be this hot girl's friend.

Fuck being friends!

We shouldn't be just friends.

Friends with benefits maybe.

Fuck buddies.

Lovers.

Girlfriend?

Fiancé even.

Maybe more.

I SHUDDER at the places that mind is going. Girlfriend, maybe. I've had a few girls who I liked enough to call my girlfriend. But fiancé? Really, Wyatt? What are you thinking? That's exactly it, though. I'm not thinking. I'm just feeling.

12

BRIELLE

I don't know why the fuck I ever insisted on being friends with Wyatt. The friends status was supposed to protect me. It was supposed to make me feel safe and to make me feel as if nothing is going to happen between us. I thought that it would create distance between us and release some of the tension that forms whenever we occupy the same room. But it's only making things worse.

I want him.

I want him to want me.

He does. I can feel it. But he won't make a move. He made me a promise and he's keen on keeping it.

Even now, standing on this stupid chair, taping tape onto the glass to stop the damn birds from crashing into it every day, I feel Wyatt's eyes burning a hole in my back pocket.

He's staring at my ass and, the scary thing is that I want him to. But more than that. I want him to grab it and pull me up to his lap and kiss me.

Of course, he won't. He has made a promise.

So now it's all up to me. And I'm afraid. And I'm a coward.

AFTER I TAPED ALL the spots where birds have crashed into the past week, I get down and sit next to him on the couch, which has become his home. Wyatt hasn't moved much in weeks. He pretends that he's fine, but I can feel his anxiety growing.

"I need to get the hell out of here. Out of this room. Away from this couch. I want to see Sebastian again."

I get goosebumps at the thought. Sebastian is the crazy, untamed, four-year-old stallion that broke both of his legs the last time he tried to ride him. I don't want Wyatt anywhere near him. He was lucky to get out of that situation with only both legs broken. The doctors said it could've been much worse. He could've broken his back and ended up like Christopher Reeves.

"Can I ask you something?" I ask.

Wyatt nods and waits for the question.

"Why did you ever get on him, in the first place? What were you trying to prove?"

I don't know much about horses, but I do know that no one in their right mind rides stallions. All the testosterone makes them crazy and wild. Unbroken.

"Nothing," he shrugs in the casual way that makes me swoon. "I just felt like riding him, that's all."

I don't believe him. "I don't think so," I say staring straight into Wyatt's deep eyes.

"You don't? Why?"

"I think you were angry with yourself. And you wanted to, I don't know, take some of that anger out on yourself."

Wyatt's eyes meet mine. I can tell by the way he sits back in the couch and adjusts his stature that I've hit on something.

"Oh please," he shrugs and rolls his eyes. He's lying. Either to just me or to the both of us.

"No, I do," I smile. "Really."

Then his face grows serious. The casualness that just danced across it all but disappears.

"Listen, Brielle," Wyatt says. All I hear is the irritation in his voice. "Please don't psychoanalyze me, okay? I've been through that enough with a ton of real doctors. The last thing I need is some more psycho babble from some novice."

His words sting. More than that even. They pierce my heart. I feel tears bubbling up and I'm about to let them all out.

"Fuck you," I say and leave before I show even more vulnerability.

"Brielle, I'm sorry. I'm sorry," I hear Wyatt yell after me, but I don't turn around. At this moment, I hate him. I hate him the way I never hated anyone.

WE DON'T SPEAK the rest of the day. By the next day, my anger with Wyatt dissipates a bit. He apologizes again and, this time, I accept his apology. By the afternoon, we joke and laugh like before. I'm glad that things between us have improved, but I am still keenly aware of the boundaries that separate us. Now, I'm also more cautious. Certain things can't be talked about or joked about.

That afternoon, over a very late lunch or an early dinner, I ask Wyatt about his family. He tells me about his domineering father and the pharmaceutical company that he started when all the kids were little.

"My father's got four kids, but that company was his real baby," he says. "And we all knew that for many years."

"What about your mom?" I ask.

"Mom was there and not there. She had her own commitments, but most of the time she was absent. It's like she had her own interests that none of us kids ever fit into."

"Not even Ophelia?" I ask. I know that mothers can often be closer to their daughters than to their sons.

"Not even O. We've all had nannies, though, so that was supposed to make up for everything, I guess. It felt like they loved me, all of us, I mean, in their own way, but it was somehow never enough. You know?"

I nod. I try to understand, but Wyatt and I come from two completely different worlds.

"What about you?" he asks. "What was it like for you growing up?"

I take a moment to consider the question.

"It wasn't really easy," I say. "My father left when I was little when my little sister was only two."

"I didn't know you had siblings."

"I don't. Well, not anymore. I never know how to answer that question about brothers or sisters."

"What do you mean?" he asks. He moves closer to me with a steadfast look of concern on his face.

"Well, I used to have a sister until I was fifteen, but then she died. She was sick almost her whole little life and, after she passed, my mother was never the same after that."

"What did she die of?" he asks even though I have the feeling that he already knows.

"Cancer. What else?" I shrug.

"Like your mother?" he gasps.

I nod. "My mom was diagnosed soon after. Right when I graduated from high school. That's why I never went to college. She was the sole breadwinner and, after her diagnosis, she couldn't really work. Not with all the chemo and radiation. So I got a job at the diner. And then another one at the bar. And I've been sort of stuck there ever since."

I look at him. I like the way he looks at me. There's pity and sorrow on his face, but it isn't as depressing as the looks other people typically have.

"But it's okay now," I smile. "Thanks largely to you."

"I just wish that I'd met you earlier," he says.

A big part of me wishes that too. I've spent so many years being poor and living paycheck to paycheck, on even less than a paycheck, that having money seemed like an answer to all of my problems. People like to say that money is not the answer to all of your problems, but for many years it would've been the answer to all of mine.

We share more this day than any other day. I feel us growing closer and closer. Even if we don't fully comprehend or understand or conceptualize each other's childhood experiences, we are at least aware of them.

After we finish our salads, Mr. Whitewater brings us soup. I hand Wyatt his bowl and take mine. It's not very comfortable to eat soup on the couch, but I don't want to move.

"What did you want to be when you grew up?" Wyatt asks.

"I don't know," I say. "You mean for work? I thought I'd be lucky if I became a nurse or something like that. It would give me a steady job or profession. The pay is much better than a waitress's."

"No," he shakes his head. "That's not what I mean. Not just for work. Didn't you have dreams of what you wanted to do or to be when you were older? No matter how unrealistic."

I smile. I'm about to tell him that only wealthy or privileged kids spend their days thinking about unrealistic dreams and go about pursuing those. But then I really think about it and realize that I, too, had a dream once. And, perhaps, still do.

"Okay, I'll tell you, but only if you promise to keep it a secret."

"Keep it a secret? Don't you know that dreams can't become a reality unless you verbalize it? Unless you infuse them with the power of speech?"

"Actually, no, I didn't know that. But if you want to hear this then you have to promise."

He takes a moment. Then agrees.

"I've never told anyone this before, but I want to be a writer," I say.

"That's great! That's an amazing thing to want to be," Wyatt smiles with his whole face.

I feel overwhelmed by his exuberance.

"But why don't you want anyone to know? It's so inspiring and beautiful!"

Inspiring and beautiful? I'm not so sure.

"Because it's embarrassing," I mumble.

"What? How?"

I stare at him. "I just don't think you understand because you were probably raised to think that you can be anyone you want. Do anything you want. Right? But I wasn't. I don't even have a bachelor's degree, Wyatt.

Only a high school diploma. I'm practically illiterate in the writing world."

"That's crap! Don't say that. Degrees don't matter. All that matters is whether or not you want to do it. And then you gotta take steps to do it."

"That's your privileged upbringing talking," I joke.

"No, it's not," he leans closer to me. His face gets really serious. "To be a writer you need heart. And you have that. I think you can be a writer. No, I *know* you can."

His words wash over me like a wave. Overwhelmed by his support and encouragement, I have trouble taking a full breath. A knot forms in the back of my throat. If I don't inhale slowly, I'm afraid that I won't be able to take a full breath again.

No one has ever believed in me so much before.

We both return to our food. Wyatt takes two last scoops of the soup. I lean across him to put the bowl on his side of the side table.

I've done this hundreds of times over the last six weeks. But today is different. There's a warmth emanating from Wyatt, the kind that I haven't felt since our last kiss. I watch him take a breath and inhale the world around us, the way people smell a bouquet of flowers.

When he opens his eyes, he catches me staring at him and sits back. He's giving me room to collect myself. He's respecting my boundaries and the rules that we have both agreed to play by. But this time, I don't, can't, respect those boundaries anymore. This time, I don't pull away. I look at his sweet, beautiful lips and press mine to them.

Immediately, his lips respond to mine. He pulls me closer to him and wraps his arms around my shoulders. In a split second, the whole world fades away. His hands move through my hair and my fingers run along his jawline. It's strong and powerful and touching it makes me want him even more.

"This is wrong," I whisper without pulling away.

"Yes, and yet it's so right," he mumbles.

And then suddenly, he stops and looks at me.

"Do you want to stop?" he asks. "Is that what you meant?"

Yes and no. I don't know.

He waits for me to answer. But I've lost the ability to speak. Instead, I reach up to him again and run my tongue on the inside of his mouth.

"Oh Brielle," he moans. He lifts up my head with his hands and then runs his hands down to my hips.

With one swift motion, he lifts me up and places me on top of him.

I laugh and continue kissing him. I feel how hard he is and it makes me feel all tingly all over my body. He pulls away from my lips and starts to kiss down my neck. I tilt my head back and sigh from pleasure. His lips make his way down my collarbone and then toward my breasts. He takes one of my breasts in his hand and kisses the top.

I close my eyes. I want this moment to last forever.

"Oh my, I'm so sorry!" a female voice shatters our bliss. I pull away from Wyatt but remain firmly on top of him.

"What the fuck are you doing here, O?" Wyatt yells out. His deep voice startles me and I fall to the side. I scramble to adjust my clothes. When everything seems in place, I look back up.

There's a tall, gorgeous woman in five- inch heels standing before me. Her hair is jet black and cut in an aggressive slant. Her makeup is flawless and her eyeslashes are long and powerful. She has pale skin and her blood red lipstick makes her look like something of a clash between a 50's pinup and a vampire.

"I live here, too, remember?" she laughs and tosses her hair. "Besides, I've come to see how you were feeling. And from what I can see, you're doing quite well."

Neither Wyatt nor I say a word. I probably look as dumbfounded as he does.

"Well, since my brother seems to have forgotten his manners, I'll introduce myself. I'm Ophelia, Wyatt's older sister."

Ophelia extends her hand to me. When I shake it, what strikes me most about it is how cold it is. Her fingers are long and her long gray nails are filed down to a point at the end. In fact, come to think of it, everything about Ophelia is pointy. She has pointy heels, a pointy nose, pointy nails, and even pointy elbows.

"I'm Brielle. I'm Wyatt's personal assistant," I mumble.

"Yes, I see. You're definitely assisting him on a very personal level," she says lifting one of her eyebrows.

"O, please. Play nice," Wyatt says. "Brielle's a friend."

Ophelia puts her sunglasses back over her eyes, turns on her heel and waves her hand. "Well, I gotta get my bag."

Wyatt and I watch her walk out. Before she reaches the end of the hallway, she turns around briefly and says, "Brielle, can you help me with something here?"

I look at Wyatt, unsure as to what to do.

"No, O, take care of it yourself," he yells back.

"No, it's okay," I get up. "I'll help her, it's no problem."

DEAR READER

Enjoyed reading

The Debt (Book Two of Wild Brothers)? Can't wait to find out what happens next?

Just click here to get your copy (ebook, print or audio):

http://www.charlotte-byrd.com/the-debt/

Thanks for reading!

Love,

Charlotte Byrd

ADVANCED READER TEAM

Sign up for Charlotte Byrd's mailing list and get notifications of New Releases, access to exclusive giveaways, and a chance to be on her Advanced Reader Team:

http://eepurl.com/btLdbT

You will only receive e-mails about new releases and you can opt out anytime

BOOKS BY CHARLOTTE BYRD

Billionaire Matchmaker Series
(standalone novels)
1. Malibu Connection - out now
2. The Date - out now

WILD BROTHERS SERIES (both standalone novels)
1. Falling for the CEO - out now
2. The Debt - out now

ONE SEMESTER SERIES (both standalone novels)
1. One Semester - out now
2. Accidental Wedding - out now

Other Books
Wrong for Me - out now

**ALL BOOKS ARE available on Amazon, Apple, Barnes & Noble, Kobo, Scribd, and all major retailers.

Printed in Great Britain
by Amazon